WINTER'S PASSION

Talon Winter Legal Thriller #6

STEPHEN PENNER

ISBN: 9798218027209

Winter's Passion

Joy Lorton, Editor.
Cover design by Nathan Wampler Book Covers.

WINTER'S PASSION

The law is reason, free from passion.

~Aristotle

CHAPTER 1

"Do you have that fire in your belly?"

Talon Winter, Attorney at Law, raised her eyebrow at the question. "Excuse me?"

The man across the desk balled up his fist and shook it in front of his stomach. Talon found his entire appearance off-putting. He wore a tailored shirt, with French cuffs and large, shiny cufflinks, and a silk tie with some sort of neo-paisley pattern. His suitcoat had an expensive sheen to it, and draped on a hanger that in turn hung from the stand-alone coatrack behind him. Wire-rimmed glasses sat on a face with thin lips and a weak chin. His hair was too long for its cut and his shoulders were too narrow for his anachronistic suspenders.

"That fire in your belly," he repeated, through clenched teeth that Talon presumed were meant to seem fierce. "That passion for the law. Do you have that, Talon Winter?"

Talon sighed slightly through her nose. She was sitting in the office of Jason Smerk, managing partner at Smerk+Nordblum, a boutique Tacoma law firm specializing in high-value plaintiffs' personal injury litigation. Smerk had a corner office with a view of Commencement Bay, and Smerk+Nordblum had the case against the Commencement Bay Yacht Club. The case brought by the Puyallup Tribe of Indians—Talon's tribe. The case she had volunteered to help litigate after the attorneys for the yacht club tried to recruit her as a token. But rather than working closely with the leadership of the Tribe, as she had expected, she found herself working far too closely with Jason Smerk.

"I have a passion for winning," Talon answered.

Talon didn't bother measuring Smerk's reaction to her comment. She didn't care about the opinion of another mediocre White man. Which was another problem she had with Jason Smerk.

"And I have a passion for my tribe."

Smerk knew at least to take a moment before responding. He was as White as they came. His freckles had freckles. But regardless of his ethnicity, he was the managing partner of the law firm Talon's tribe had decided to hire to get their land—well, a small sliver of their land—back from the Commencement Bay Yacht Club. Smerk leaned forward and nodded, his expression turned solemn.

"I share that passion, Talon," he assured in a tone she found very unassuring. "That's why you're here. That's why we agreed to associate with an attorney who's not in our firm. But that's why I need to know." Again, the fist in front of his stomach. "Do you have that fire in the belly?"

Talon sighed and stifled an eye roll. "Sure, Jason. Whatever."

Smerk took a moment, holding his posture and expression as he considered whether to settle for Talon's words, or admit to the feeling behind them. After another moment, he nodded and sat back. "Good," he said, taking the win. "Very good. Excellent."

Talon restrained herself from making a thesaurus joke.

"I need to know your heart is truly and verily in this

litigation," Smerk continued, "if you're going to sit in our client meeting this afternoon."

"Client meeting?" Talon repeated. Maybe there was a fire in her belly after all. Or at least some excitement at actually getting to sit down with someone from the Tribe and strategize the case. The closest she'd gotten to anyone at the Tribe was when she would drive by the new resort complex on her way toward downtown. The parking garage alone was as large as the entire old resort had been. She relished a chance to thank them personally for the opportunity to help them.

"Yes," Smerk confirmed. "At three o'clock."

Talon checked the time. It was 1:20. Plenty of time to get prepared for—

"So you'd better hurry," Smerk continued, "if you want to get back in time."

Talon frowned. "Back from where?"

Smerk slid a bundle of papers across his desk to her. "The courthouse. This is our response to the yacht club's latest discovery motion. Well, actually, it's our reply to their response to our motion to compel discovery—"

Talon put up a hand. During her years after becoming a criminal defense attorney, she had managed to forget how much she hated the civil procedure rules. She didn't want to be reminded of them any more than was absolutely necessary. "Got it."

"It's due today," Smerk went on. "The meeting is at three and the courthouse closes at four-thirty. This needs to be filed before the meeting, if you're going to make the meeting."

Talon frowned slightly. "Can't we use a courier? Or one of the legal assistants?"

"Fire," Smerk responded. "Belly. Show me you care enough about this case to get your hands dirty, and I'll show you how much

I appreciate it by letting you shake hands with the client."

Talon's hands had gotten plenty dirty since she left civil practice to pursue a career in criminal defense. Dirty with the blood of her enemies. Prosecutors and cops and even judges who dared to underestimate her, or who estimated her fairly but couldn't stop her anyway. Filing a reply to a response to a motion to force someone to answer some question? That was the kind of thing she would use to wipe off those dirty hands of hers.

Still, discretion was the better part of valor, and Smerk, as managing partner, could definitely block her from attending the client meeting. But the real reason she stood up and snatched the papers off of his desk was that she was dying to set foot in the courthouse again. Talon Winter in a corporate office was a tiger in a cage. If that tiger wasn't allowed to make a kill, at least she could stalk her old hunting grounds.

"See you at three, Jason."

CHAPTER 2

The Pierce County Courthouse wasn't actually called that. It was named 'The County-City Building.' It housed more than just the courts: the county council, the county executive, and the county sheriff's headquarters were all within its walls. The only 'city' part seemed to be the Tacoma Municipal Court, which was really a vote for the 'courthouse' moniker. The rest of the city government was a few blocks east, down the hill and toward the water, and it had been more than a decade since Tacoma P.D. left for their new headquarters in the south part of town. But regardless of its other tenants, The 'C.C.B.' was home to the Pierce County Superior Court, and its clerk's office, where Talon needed to file Smerk+Nordblum's reply to the response to the motion to force the other side to just answer the damn questions already.

Talon supposed the 'County-City Building' name was appropriate as she walked toward the main entrance. It didn't look anything like a courthouse. It screamed government building from 1959. It looked like two cardboard boxes, an upright one stacked on top of one that fell over. The clerk of the court's office was on the third floor of the upright box.

There weren't even any courthouse steps. Just a large, flat

cement entryway that was too wide to be a sidewalk, but too narrow to be a plaza. It was big enough for a car, however. Several years prior, a disaffected citizen, presumably upset with a ruling he had lost inside, drove his car over the cement approach and directly into the front doors of the building. Since then, the not-quite-a-plaza was set off from the road by three waist-high concrete pillars spaced slightly less than a standard car-width apart. It was as she reached those memorials to how much hatred some people could feel toward the justice system, that Talon was reminded why that was the case.

To either side of the concrete, there were small grassy areas with some low bushes. And just as government buildings attracted crazy and/or desperate people who wanted to crash their cars into the courthouse for taking away their kids or their homes or whatever else they were losing via The System, such buildings also attracted crazy and/or desperate people who just wanted a place to sit down for a few minutes. Or lay down. Or maybe sleep in the middle of the day.

If the County-City Building had indeed been just the courthouse, that sort of behavior might have been overlooked, at least temporarily. Maybe even permanently, like in that larger city to the north. Courthouses were filled with the mentally ill and chemically dependent. A few more on the lawn out front was little more than overflow. But the County Executive and the County Councilmembers had to use that entrance as well, and it simply wouldn't do to allow any human reminders of failed policies and blind eyes.

As a result, the police were routinely sent out to round up the derelicts, and they were routinely none too gentle about it. Certainly not right then, as Talon approached the unfolding confrontation.

"Get up now!" one of three burly officers was yelling at the man curled up on the grass, his arms wrapped around his head. "Or you will be arrested!"

Talon frowned. She was no fan of cops, but at least they were giving the poor guy a chance before laying hands on him. If the man stood up and walked away, that would probably be the end of it. She hoped so. She had other things to do.

The officer reached down and grabbed the man's upper arm. Talon wasn't always one to bring race into things, but she also knew it was already in a lot more things than some people were willing to admit, or even able to see. As it stood, the man on the ground was Black, the officer grabbing him with one hand and the other on his gun was White, and of the two officers providing backup to that primary aggressor, one was White and one was Black. But all three of them were cops, and all three of them were covered in body armor and weapons, just to deal with a mentally ill and/or intoxicated man trying to take a nap.

"On your feet now!" the grabbing officer ordered as he jerked the man's body toward the sky. "Or you will be tased!"

That seems a bit excessive, Talon thought. She decided she was going to say something. But someone beat her to it.

"Hey, Mr. White Police Officer!" a woman yelled from a car that had just pulled up in front of the not-courthouse. "Let go of that Black man! He's not doing anything!"

The woman herself was Black and leaning out of the driver's side of her late model minivan. She was probably about 30 years old, with natural hair, hoop earrings, and a cell phone in her hand.

"I'm filming you, Mr. Officer!" she called out. "Don't you do anything to that man. I'm filming all of you."

Talon smiled. As much as some cops loved bullying the weak, that's how much they hated getting caught doing it.

"Turn that camera off!" the other White officer yelled at her, temporarily turning his attention away from their primary victim. He stepped toward the woman with one hand raised and the other hovering over his gun. "Turn that off right now or you will be arrested for obstruction of justice."

Technically, it's called obstruction of a law enforcement officer, Talon thought to herself, *but most cops don't think there's a difference.*

Talon was about to insert herself into the situation, perhaps announcing herself as the lawyer for either or both of the people the police were currently yelling at, but then three things happened that prevented that course of action.

First, the officer trying to drag the man out of the bushes dropped said man and sprinted toward the driver filming them.

Second, the driver stomped on the gas and peeled away from the curb.

Third, Talon's phone rang. She looked at her screen. It was Smerk. Eye roll.

Talon answered the phone and put it to her ear, but her eyes were filled with the scene unfolding in front of her on Tacoma Avenue.

"Have you filed that response yet?"

The officer who had ordered her to stop filming sprinted after the vehicle, trailing behind her on the roadway.

"It's a reply, not a response," Talon corrected.

The officer who dropped the homeless man to rush her vehicle took off down the sidewalk, trying to head her off at the proverbial pass, it appeared.

"Whatever," Smerk huffed. "Is it filed?"

The third officer remained standing next to the half-sleeping man, watching his colleagues pursue the woman who dared to document nothing more than what they were actually doing.

"Not quite," Talon answered. "I'm just outside the courthouse."

"It's the County-City Building, not the courthouse," Smerk corrected her back in a schoolyard sing-song.

"Right," Talon agreed, but her focus was what was transpiring at the end of the street.

The driver took a hard left, tires squealing. As she did so, the officer on the sidewalk reached the corner and jumped directly into the path of the vehicle. The driver slammed on her brakes, narrowly avoiding the cop. The other officer reached her car then. He threw open the door and pulled the driver from the vehicle by her hair, face first into the pavement.

"Get it filed now," Smerk whined. "The Tribe had to reschedule the meeting. It's moved up to two o'clock. You have fifteen minutes to get that filed and get back here or we do the meeting without you. I'm not letting you walk in late."

Talon frowned. Patrol cars with flashing lights and wailing sirens were already showing up to assist the capture of the oh so dangerous criminal who dared to film police officers and then not run one of them over despite his best efforts. It was all over but the falsified police report and trumped-up charges.

"I'll be there in ten," Talon grumbled. "Save my seat at the conference table."

CHAPTER 3

It actually took Talon thirteen minutes to get the reply filed and back to Smerk+Nordblum's offices, but that was fast enough to secure her spot at the far end of the remarkably long conference table, as far away as possible from the delegation from the Puyallup Tribe of Indians. She had managed to get back in time to take that one and only open seat, but the time for handshakes and introductions had passed. Maybe afterward. But right then, it was time to get down to business.

"We are concerned with the pace of the litigation," began the woman at the opposite end of the table from Talon. There were three representatives from the Tribe, one man and two women. The man was a bit older, probably in his 50s, with short hair and wrinkles at the edges of his face. The women were both younger, probably in their 30s, like Talon, dressed sharply, like Talon, with keen eyes and confidence that floated around them like an aura. Like Talon. "We'd like a progress report."

Talon was eager for a progress report too. She'd signed on months ago, but it appeared, judging by her quest to the courthouse, that they were still bogged down in discovery. Having to argue some motions to get the other side to answer questions was to be expected in any civil litigation, but the yacht club was trying to slow things to an absolute crawl. Talon understood why; the longer things took, the longer they kept the land. But Talon came to kick ass and take names, not beg a judge to order a yacht club owner to turn over its bank statements.

Talon turned to Jason Smerk and rested her chin on her hand, awaiting his answer.

"Things are progressing apace," he began. Typical lawyer. Lots of words meaning nothing. "We appreciate your confidence in our services."

The other woman frowned. "We want to be confident in your services, but we've received too few progress reports about too little progress." Talon liked her. Her long black hair was twisted back into a tight ponytail. "We've been trying to get this land back for generations now, literally. We know how to be patient. But we also know there's a time when patience has to give way to action."

"And results," the first woman put in. Her hair fell loosely over her shoulders. "This is about results. It's not for headlines and publicity. We have plans for that land. Plans to benefit the entire Tribe. Every day it remains in the wrong hands is a day our members go without those benefits."

Talon decided to speak up. She waved a hand at Smerk. "Jason, may I?"

She didn't wait for an answer; they both knew she wouldn't like it.

"I'm one of those members," Talon said. "I share your desire—our desire—to win this case and win it now. That's why I'm here, and that's what we're going to do. As soon as we get over this next discovery hurdle, we will make sure it's the last discovery hurdle."

"How are you going to do that?" The man finally spoke,

leaning forward to await Talon's response.

"Yeah," Smerk added with a thinly veiled sneer, "how are you going to do that?"

"Easy," Talon answered. "The best way to stop arguing over whether they answer our questions is to stop asking questions."

"I'm sorry." Smerk blinked almost audibly. "What?

"Discovery is a tool," Talon explained, "not an end unto itself. We don't need to read every statement of every account since they incorporated. We already know they've made a bunch of money off our land. That's not in question, and it's irrelevant. It's a violation of a hundred-and-fifty-year-old treaty and a thirty-year-old land claim settlement; it's not about how much they have or haven't made off that land. We're not asking for a cut of the profits—although we should probably do that too—we're asking for the land back. Demanding. And you don't ask permission to demand something, especially when you're in the right."

The three visitors looked at each other and nodded with obvious approval.

Smerk, on the other hand, obviously did not approve.

"Yes, well, of course it's not quite as simple as that," he laughed nervously. "We don't want to go into trial unprepared. You never know what will happen at trial."

Talon shrugged. "You kind of do. I mean, the facts are the facts. The law is the law. Sure, there might be some inconsistencies once actual people get on the stand and give actual testimony, but that's the fun part. Waiting for those inconsistencies, recognizing them, and exploiting them. But we can't do that until we get this thing to trial."

She could tell Smerk was about to argue with her, so she kept talking.

"When I started doing criminal defense work, I was stunned

by how many defense attorneys would agree to waive their clients' right to a speedy trial. For 'further negotiations', they would say. As if the prosecutor was really going to negotiate anything so long as there was no threat of an actual trial he might lose. They would let their clients sit in jail, unable to post bail, while they delayed the case for months, even years, to beg for a plea deal that was never coming."

Talon shook her head. "That's not how you do it. The way you do it is that you demand a speedy trial, you demand the State actually bring their witnesses to court, and you demand it now. Nothing focuses a bully's mind like having to fight an actual fight. That's all prosecutors are: bullies. And that's all those fat cats at the Commencement Bay Yacht Club are. They're bullies. And they will walk all over us if we let them."

Smerk laughed again, nervously, humorlessly. Talon was pretty confident she was about to be kicked off the case. But at least she'd spoken her mind.

"I'm sure we all appreciate your enthusiasm, Ms. Winter," Smerk condescended, "but this isn't one of your quick and dirty criminal cases. This is—"

"Put her in charge," the woman with the ponytail said. "What's your name again, Ms. ...?"

"Winter," she answered. "Talon Winter."

"Nice to meet you, Ms. Winter," she said. "I'm Charlotte Draper, general counsel for the Tribe." She looked again to Smerk. "Put Ms. Winter in charge."

Smerk was gobsmacked. "Um, well, you see, I'm the managing partner, and—"

"Put Ms. Winter in charge of this case," Charlotte Draper directed, "or we will find another firm and you will lose all of those billable hours you love to charge us every month."

Smerk grimaced. He looked from the woman giving him orders to the woman who had just stolen the case out from under him. He probably shouldn't have let her in on the meeting after all, Talon supposed. Finally, he forced a broad smile and threw his hand wide. "Of course! Of course. Ms. Winter is an excellent trial attorney. One of the best, I hear."

The best, Talon thought, but she didn't feel the need to give voice to it just then. It felt understood.

"That's why she's here, right?" Smerk continued through clenched teeth. "That, and she's a member of your tribe so she got to just ask her way onto a multimillion-dollar litigation. A multimillion-dollar litigation she just got put in charge of. That's fine. This is fine. Everything is fine."

Talon knew Smerk didn't really think it was fine, but that was okay with her. Agree to disagree.

"Thank you, Ms. Draper," Talon spoke up. "It's been an honor to meet you. And it's even more of an honor to be entrusted with the stewardship of this case."

"Of course it is, Ms. Winter." Draper smiled, but sharply. "Please don't disappoint us."

CHAPTER 4

Talon hurried out of the meeting and directly to her car. She may have had a workspace at Smerk+Nordblum, but her real office was in a building on the other side of downtown. Past downtown, actually. Filled with a ragtag assortment of solo practitioners like herself, both lawyers and other professions, each just trying to hustle enough to make rent. That was where she belonged.

Also, she didn't really want to talk to Smerk immediately after stealing the case from him. She could summon him to a meeting later in the week. The thought pleased her.

She drove out of the parking lot and made her way down to where Pacific Avenue became Schuster Parkway, along the water to her small but familiar office building, filled with people who knew her and liked her anyway. Or maybe even more than liked. Talon knew it was wrong, cruel almost, but after a stressful afternoon of taking over cases and watching innocent people be assaulted by the police, there was an undeniable solace in being in the company of a man whose painfully obvious love she could blithely unrequite.

"Curt?" she called out as she approached his office door, two floors down from her own, at her insistence. "You in? I've got an amazing story to tell you. Two, in fact. Maybe three, if I remember something else."

Curt Fairchild, private investigator, friend, one time lover—only one time and it was her decision and she wasn't ever going to decide that again so he really needed to get over it—was in. He was also not alone.

"Talon!" Curt jumped to his feet at the sight of her. It wasn't a bad sight for her either. Curt was fit and handsome, with thick black hair and a muscular frame under his snug shirt. But his friend…

"Hey, Curt," she managed a greeting. She'd already forgotten why she'd come into Curt's office but she was glad she had. "Who's your friend?"

His friend was, in a word, hot. And handsome. And hot. He also had thick black hair, but it had a wave to it and flowed back from his strong jaw and high cheekbones. His nose was especially handsome, with a notch at the bridge that dared you to find it anything but sexy. Curt was fit, but this guy was ripped. He stood up to shake Talon's hand in his large, manly grip, looked down at her with emerald green eyes, and flashed not just a winning, but a championship smile.

"I'm Zack Claymore."

"You certainly are," Talon replied as her hand melted into Zack Claymore's. "I'm Talon. Talon Winter. It's a pleasure to meet you."

"The pleasure's all mine," Zack replied. He flashed that grin at Curt. "Is this the Talon you were telling me about?"

Curt smiled too, but an awkward grimace. "Um, yeah."

"There aren't too many of us," Talon offered. "But I'm pretty sure he's never mentioned you. I think I would have remembered."

"Zack's my best friend from high school," Curt explained. "He lives in Portland now, but is in town for a visit."

The thought of Zack Claymore leaving soon was both disappointing and appealing. What happens with the guy from Portland can leave with him to Portland.

"How long are you in town, Zack?" she asked.

"The conference runs through Friday, then I thought I'd stay through the weekend," Zack answered. He smiled at her again. "Maybe longer. I've got some flexibility."

Flexibility meant no wife and kids. Good. Or maybe no real career. Bad.

"Conference, huh?" Talon asked. "What line of work are you in? You're not a private investigator too, are you?"

Another awkward grin from Curt.

"Oh, no," Zack answered. "I'm a firefighter."

Talon looked again at his frame. *Of course you are.*

"But that's not why I'm in town," he went on "I run a non-profit for at-risk youth. The West Coast chapter of our national organization is holding its annual conference in Seattle this year."

"A non-profit?" Talon repeated. "For at-risk youth? And you're a firefighter in your day job?" She glanced around the room. "Is there a camera somewhere? Where's the camera?"

Curt's eyebrows knitted together. "I don't have a camera in my office."

Talon rolled her eyes. When they lowered again, Zack met them, his own smiling. "We should grab a drink, Talon Winter. Curt says you know all the best places in Tacoma."

"He did?"

"I did?"

"Well, no," Zack admitted. "But I bet you do, right?"

Talon allowed a sly smile to settle into the corner of her mouth. "Of course I do."

CHAPTER 5

Almost as ridiculous as filing a motion to force someone to answer a question was holding a full court hearing with oral argument on that motion. Even more ridiculous was how worked up the lawyers got, as if talking to a judge in open court was a feat reserved for heroes of legend, rather than just, say, Thursday.

In actuality, it was Friday. All the civil motions were scheduled for Fridays so the judges could spend the rest of their weeks presiding over the real work of criminal jury trials. Talon was more than familiar with both the courthouse and the courtroom of Judge Winnifred Masters. Jason Smerk, not so much.

"Are you sure you know where we're headed?" he asked as he tried to keep up with Talon's brisk gait. "There was a directory in the lobby. I don't want to be late because we went to the wrong courtroom."

"Then follow me," Talon answered without turning back to look at him, "and go to the right courtroom."

Judge Masters's courtroom was the last one on the right at the end of a long hallway on the second floor, the top floor of the cardboard box laying on its side. Talon's heels rang off the marble floor. She was clearly in charge. The only reason Smerk wasn't carrying her briefcase was that she carried her own damned briefcase, thank you very much. She reached the courtroom door first and pulled it open. Someone observing them might have thought she had opened the door for Smerk. She hadn't. She walked in and Smerk hurried through the closing door behind her.

"What's the hurry?" he nearly panted.

"I thought you didn't want to be late," she sneered.

"I thought you said we wouldn't be," he replied, "because it was the right courtroom."

"It is," she answered. "And we aren't."

The only problem was that no one else was late either. Those Friday civil motion dockets were usually overset, crowding a dozen or more hearings into each half day. Talon and Smerk were only two of twenty or more lawyers already milling about the gallery waiting for the judge to come out and start calling cases. If both sides' lawyers were present, it was a 'matched pair' and the arguments could proceed, albeit under a strict time limit. They had to get all of the arguments and rulings done by noon, a feat made even more challenging by the fifteen-minute break the court reporter would need by the middle of the morning just to rest their hands.

Talon scanned the courtroom for her opposing counsel. As much as she would have loved to have the other side not show at all, and therefore win by default, she knew that wasn't a real possibility. She needed them there so when Judge Masters took the bench and called the case of *The Puyallup Tribe of Indians versus The Commencement Bay Yacht Club, LLC*, they could immediately step up to the bar and argue the motion. If the other side wasn't there, they'd get 'footed' and have to wait until the end of the calendar, or worse, get set over to one o'clock if the other cases took up the entire morning. Talon didn't have time for that. But luckily, her opposing counsel was easy to spot and he was definitely there, seated in the exact middle of the first row.

Peter Grainsley was the namesake partner of The Grainsley Firm, a high-powered boutique law firm that normally specialized in class-action plaintiff work, especially consumer product liability and mass transportation tragedies. Think airplane crashes and school buses off a cliff. Being an expert in suing people, he also knew how to defend high-profile lawsuits. Throw in the fact that he parked his 60-foot yacht at the Commencement Bay Yacht Club, and he was the one the yacht club's Seattle law firm—Erickson, Larson and Sondheim—turned to when their efforts to recruit had Talon failed. They had wanted her for the optics of a Native woman defending a lawsuit brought by her own tribe, but once she realized what they were doing, Talon turned them down flat. Grainsley didn't bring that type of optics, but he had his own unmistakable look, one that was fully on display when he felt Talon's gaze on his neck, and stood up to confront his opponents.

Grainsley was 6′ 8″ and well over 300 pounds, with a bright pink bald head and piercing blue eyes under wispy white eyebrows. His light gray suit was specially tailored—it had to be—of the highest quality fabric. His silk tie probably cost more than Talon's entire outfit. His face was pale and doughy, and unfurled into a cold smile as he lumbered over to them and looked down at Talon and her companion.

"You must be the new lawyer Smerk was talking about the last time he lost a motion to me." Grainsley's deep voice almost shook the room. "The Great Red Hope."

Talon took a beat to make sure she'd heard what she'd just heard. "Excuse me? What did you just say?"

"I've heard good things about you." Grainsley ignored her question. "Well, good and bad. Good lawyer. Bad person. Kind of a bitch, that's what I heard. That's probably what makes you a good lawyer, too, though, am I right?"

"Wow. So, you're just an asshole," Talon answered. "I'm going to enjoy showing you just how good of a lawyer I am."

Grainsley laughed, a deep grating guffaw that drew the attention of everyone in the courtroom. "The little lady is trying to be a big man. Okay, little lady, let's see what you got." He jabbed a thick finger into Smerk's face. "Let's see if you can get the judge to order me to do more than this guy has managed over these last two years."

Smerk probably should have said something to defend his honor—Talon certainly wasn't going to—but Talon spoke first, and not about Smerk.

"You'll see what I do when I do it. And you won't see it coming."

Grainsley grinned at that. His teeth were yellow and crooked. Before he could decide on a response, the judge entered the courtroom and any further conversation was aborted by the bailiff's call.

"All rise! The Pierce County Superior Court is now in session, The Honorable Winnifred Masters presiding!"

Judge Masters took her seat above the litigants. She was in her 50s, with gray streaks in her black curls, and large glasses in front of wise eyes. "You may be seated."

Grainsley threw one more smug grin at Talon, then returned to his seat at the front of the courtroom.

"I hate that guy," Smerk hissed under his breath.

Talon supposed he would. Talon wasn't going to waste time feeling anything toward yet another entitled, racist, sexist asshole. She was just going to beat him.

"Do we have any matched pairs?" Judge Masters asked. She

was speaking to her bailiff, but Talon spoke up from the back of the courtroom.

"The parties are ready on the matter of the *The Puyallup Tribe of Indians versus The Commencement Bay Yacht Club*, Your Honor." Talon called out. "Talon Winter appearing on behalf of the Tribe."

Smerk bumped her arm.

"Oh, and Jason Smerk appearing as well," she added.

"No," he whispered. "I mean, don't yell out like that. Now the judge is going to be irritated with us. It's going to be that much harder to win."

Talon smiled at his silly little concern. He really had no idea what her plan was. Luckily, neither did Grainsley. And it didn't matter if Masters did.

Judge Masters didn't seem fazed by Talon's outburst. She might not have smiled at it, but she didn't frown either. And she acquiesced.

"All right then," the judge said. "Let's call the matter of *The Puyallup Tribe of Indians versus The Commencement Bay Yacht Club*."

Grainsley pushed himself to his feet again—no small task—and Talon took a step toward the bar.

Smerk grabbed her arm. "Maybe I should argue this. I wrote the brief after all."

Talon offered the faintest of smiles. "I'll argue it, Jason. It's my case now."

Smerk was still holding her arm. "Well, did you read my briefing? Do you know what to argue?"

Talon's smile blossomed a bit. "I know what to argue, Jason. Now let go of my arm. People are beginning to stare."

Smerk's eyes darted around the courtroom as he released his grasp. Talon marched forward and met Grainsley at the bar. He took up the space of two people and Talon had to resist the urge to step away from him. She had her assigned place in front of the judge and she didn't want to be seen giving even an inch to her opponent.

"This is the Tribe's motion, I believe," Judge Masters began, "so I will hear first from counsel for the Tribe. Ms. Winter it is, I believe?"

One of the perks of doing criminal work was being in court so much that all the judges learned your name. She'd never done a trial in front of Judge Masters, but she had done plenty of other preliminary hearings in front of every judge in the county.

"And then I will hear from Mr. Grainsley," Masters said.

Talon supposed Grainsley wasn't the sort of person anyone forgot after encountering him even once.

"Please keep in mind," the judge continued, "we have a full docket this morning, and another equally overset docket this afternoon. I have read everyone's briefs, so you do not need to repeat orally what you have already argued in writing. Get to the point so we can get to the next case."

Fair enough, Talon agreed.

"So, with that," Judge Masters nodded to Talon, "Ms. Winter, why should I grant your motion to compel the defendant to answer your interrogatories?"

Talon nodded for a moment, then shrugged. "You probably shouldn't, Your Honor. Seems like a complete waste of time, actually."

Masters's eyebrows shot up over the rims of her glasses. Grainsley turned to stare at her. And Talon knew Smerk's head was about to explode.

"I beg your pardon?" Judge Masters said. "You want me to deny your motion? Did you actually read Mr. Smerk's brief?"

Talon guessed that was also what Smerk was thinking right

then.

"Oh yes, Your Honor, I read it," Talon answered. "And I read Mr. Grainsley's response. I even read Mr. Smerk's reply to that response before personally filing it with the court myself. As I understand the controversy, Mr. Smerk's law firm served Mr. Grainsley's law firm with a series of written questions, interrogatories. There were either twenty questions, as claimed by Mr. Smerk, or there were fifty-three questions, as claimed by Mr. Grainsley, since almost every main question included anywhere from three to five sub-questions. Mr. Grainsley argues that this violates the civil court rules limiting the number of interrogatories each side can submit to the other. Mr. Smerk replies that even if it were true that there were more than twenty questions, it shouldn't matter because Mr. Grainsley has never answered any of the previous interrogatories put to him, accusing Mr. Grainsley of frustrating discovery in an attempt to delay the litigation indefinitely so as to avoid there ever being a determination on the merits—merits which even I am having trouble remembering now after this truncated recitation of, well not the case, but the procedural gamesmanship attendant to the case."

Judge Masters had to smile down at Talon. "So, you're conceding that the interrogatories submitted by your firm exceeded the limits set by the court rules?"

Talon shook her head. "I'm conceding that Mr. Grainsley can delay the trial indefinitely by refusing to allow discovery to proceed and hiding behind technical defects and poorly drafted court rules."

"Discovery in a civil case takes time, Ms. Winter," Judge Masters remarked. "Surely you recall that from your days doing civil litigation."

Talon's reputation did precede her after all. She allowed a

small grin at that.

"I do recall that, Your Honor," she agreed, "and then I learned from my days doing criminal work that sometimes you just have to get in front of a jury and start calling witnesses. I've read the interrogatories prepared by Mr. Smerk. They are very thorough. They would have to be, with three to five sub-questions each. But not one of them really addresses the singular issue in this case: should the land that the Commencement Bay Yacht Club sits on be returned to The Puyallup Tribe of Indians? I could read every bank statement ever produced for every member of that yacht club since the day they laid the first board for the first dock, and none of that would have the slightest bearing on which sovereign has the superior claim to that stretch of coastline."

Judge Master nodded thoughtfully. "What are you suggesting then?" She asked over those glasses of hers.

"Strike the entire discovery schedule and set a trial date," Talon answered. "In thirty days. In front of Your Honor, or whatever judge is available. Let's try this case, not let it die of old age. Surely Mr. Grainsley can be ready in thirty days. And I'm ready now."

Talon felt certain that if she were to turn around she would see Smerk waving frantically at her to shut the hell up and get back to the arguments in his brief. That was one of the reasons she didn't turn around. The other reason was that she wanted to see Grainsley's reaction when she added, "Unless Mr. Grainsley is afraid of trial."

Grainsley allowed her a bemused grin. More of a snarl really. But he didn't say anything to her directly. He knew to wait for the judge to pose a question he actually had to answer. Which, of course, she did.

"What do you think of Ms. Winter's suggestion, Mr.

Grainsley?" Judge Masters asked.

"Her suggestion that the Court deny Mr. Smerk's motion to compel my clients to answer their inappropriate and unfounded interrogatories?" he replied. "We have no objection to that, Your Honor."

Judge Masters smiled. "No, Mr. Smerk. Her larger proposal. The one where discovery is deemed complete by both sides and trial begins in thirty days."

"I'm not prepared to say that we have completed our discovery process, Your Honor," Grainsley responded.

Masters nodded. "So, you still want to ask them questions?"

"Yes, Your Honor," Grainsley confirmed.

"But you don't want to answer their questions?"

Grainsley shifted his rather sizeable weight. "I will be happy to respond to discovery requests which can be shown to be in compliance with the relevant legal requirements."

"So, no," Judge Masters translated. She sighed and looked back at Talon. "I believe Ms. Winter has a point. This litigation could drag on for even more months and years if every discovery demand is subject to a full hearing in front of the judge. I suspect that if I were to rule today that Commencement Bay must answer the interrogatories submitted by the Tribe, some new issue would pop up before that could be accomplished and we would all find ourselves back here in a month from now with nothing accomplished except another round of billing to the clients."

"Your Honor, I must protest," Grainsley interjected. "I represent my client to the best of my abilities and part of that is holding the other side to the letter of the law. I will not apologize for that."

"I'm not asking you to apologize," the judge replied. "I'm also not going to order you to answer the interrogatories."

"Thank you, Your Honor." Grainsley offered a grateful nod to the judge.

"I am going to schedule this case for trial in sixty days," Judge Masters continued. "That will give both sides a bit longer than Ms. Winter suggested, if less than what Mr. Grainsley might like. The trial will be in front of me, with no further discovery required."

Talon smiled. Grainsley not so much.

"But Your Honor," he almost wailed, "we cannot possibly be ready for trial in that short of time, and there is still much discovery to be completed. There is an order to these things, Your Honor. First written interrogatories, then requests for production of documents, then depositions. You can't do a deposition until you've obtained the records you need to question the witness on, and you can't know what documents to demand until you've received the answers to your interrogatories."

"And you can't do any of that if you refuse to answer the interrogatories," Masters responded. "I am not unaware, Mr. Grainsley, that the status quo favors your client. It is Ms. Winter's client who is seeking a change of circumstances. Every day that this litigation stalls is, in effect, another day that your client wins, at least temporarily. I do not fault you for doing your job, but I have a job to do as well, and that is to see to it that cases are litigated in a timely fashion. The Tribe deserves its day in court as much as your client, and that day will be in sixty days right here in this very courtroom."

Talon finally turned around to offer a beaming grin to Smerk. He was not grinning back. In fact, his face was flushed and there was a vein bulging in his neck. Talon's grin broadened at the sight.

"I cannot begin a trial, Your Honor," Grainsley was still

arguing, "without at least deposing the opposing party."

"You want to depose the entire Puyallup Tribe of Indians?" Talon scoffed. "Cool. Can I depose the main dock of your yacht club? Maybe the dining room, too?"

"Ms. Winter has a point," Judge Masters agreed. "Both of the parties in this lawsuit are entities, not people."

"I should still be able to conduct at least one deposition," Grainsley insisted. It was almost a pout, which was a strange look on a man of his size. Like a giant baby in a suit.

"Fine," Masters agreed. "It's settled. Trial will commence in sixty days, and each side can conduct one deposition between now and then. Choose your targets carefully, counsel. I will not grant leave for additional depositions. This matter is complete."

Masters dismissed them and called out the name of the next case she was ready to address.

"Expect my summons for deposition by the end of business Monday," Grainsley tried to threaten.

"It's going to take you that long to figure out who to depose, huh?" Talon replied. "Don't strain yourself, Pete."

Grainsley sneered at her, but avoided any further verbal jousting. He rotated his gigantic frame and trundled himself toward the exit. In the breech, Smerk scurried up to Talon's side.

"What did you just do?" he lamented. "We can never be ready in sixty days."

"Of course we can," Talon answered, watching after Grainsley's retreating figure. "But I'm betting they can't."

CHAPTER 6

Smerk couldn't stop whining, even after they'd exited the courtroom. In fact, it got worse in the hallway. But Talon was done with it.

"I'll call you when I get back to the office, Jason." She put up a hand to stop the torrent of complaint spilling from his twisted mouth. "Right now I have another matter to attend to."

That stopped Smerk, at least for a moment. "What, here? In the courthouse?"

"The County-City Building," she corrected. She could forgive a civil lawyer forgetting what the building was really called. They rarely went to a courthouse after all. "And yes."

"What matter?" Smerk demanded.

Talon wasn't one to be demanded of. "I will call you when I get back to the office, Jason," she repeated. "Or maybe Monday. In the meantime, give some thought to who you think we should depose from the yacht club."

"You don't already have someone in mind?" Smerk seemed surprised.

"Of course I do," Talon was sure to answer. "But I'd like to hear who you think we should depose, before we schedule the deposition with the person I've chosen."

That also stunned Smerk into a momentary silence, so Talon

took advantage and departed, her heels clacking off the marble as she made her way to the far other side of the second floor. To where the criminal courtrooms were.

Talon did not in fact have another matter in the building. She just needed a respite from the banality of arguing about answering questions. She needed to get back to where people were negotiating cases in years of life instead of thousands of dollars, fighting The System, standing up to The Man, and bringing their best to deal with the worst people did to each other. She needed the Criminal Presiding Courtroom. She needed The Pit.

The Pit was the conference room situated between the two main felony criminal courtrooms. It was where the attorneys—prosecutors and defense alike—congregated to negotiate cases, tell dark jokes, and share pictures of their kids. It was cacophonous and crackled with the energy of the just and unjust alike. It was alive. And after that argument about how many questions can a lawyer ask to change a light bulb, Talon wanted to feel alive.

She didn't actually have a criminal case set for pretrial that morning, so there wasn't a particular prosecutor she needed to find and negotiate with. She could just take in the sights and sounds. She was hoping she might run into one of the better defense attorneys and maybe bootstrap her visit into a lunch at one of the cheap restaurants surrounding the courthouse, catering to broke criminals and almost broke government lawyers.

She let her eyes fall over the assembled crowd looking for a familiar, and cool, face, but it was her ears that found something to grab her attention.

"... and then the cop just runs out in front of her. He's lucky she stopped in time or he would have been street pizza."

"Bacon pizza!" came a reply. "You know, because cop? Pig? Bacon?"

Talon turned to see who was talking, so she could then confirm they were talking about what she thought they were talking about. It was two men, on the young side for lawyers, so late twenties, maybe thirty. Probably public defenders, judging by their clothes. Not that they were shabby, although that might have also been a tip-off given the pay rates for public defenders, but because they were on the far casual edge of what could pass for court attire. Jackets and ties, as required, but cheap ties, loosened to the point of almost unravelling, and jeans that were dark, but still jeans. Slip-on shoes and white socks. One had a mop of dark blond hair that needed a trim to stay out of his eyes; the other either couldn't find his razor that morning or was considering growing a beard that, in Talon's estimation, he probably couldn't quite pull off.

"So, wait, though," the darker one with the stubble put up a thoughtful hand, "the cop ran in front of her car, but they're threatening to charge her with assault?"

"They already did charge her with assault," the blond moppy one answered.

"Assault in the third degree?" the other asked. "Assault on a police officer?"

Blondie laughed darkly. "No, man. That's what it should be. Well, it shouldn't be anything, but if they were going to charge a felony assault, that's the one I would have thought."

"Right," Stubble answered. "A felony, but just barely. Then she's happy to plead out to a misdemeanor Assault Four."

"She'd be ecstatic to plead to an Assault Four," Blondie answered. "Or at least *I'd* be ecstatic to plead her out to it. Misdemeanor, credit for time served, next case, right? But no, they charged her—"

"Assault Two?" Stubble guessed. "Assault with a deadly weapon? They're saying the car was a deadly weapon?"

Blondie shook his head, sending the mop circling his temples. "Nope. Assault One."

"Assault in the first degree?" That stubbled jaw fell open. "That's like attempted murder."

Blondie nodded. "Yup. It's the exact same sentence range as attempted murder in the second degree."

"How do they get to Assault One?" Stubble asked, shaking his head. "I mean, how do they get to any assault with the cop jumping in front of the car, but how can they possibly charge first degree?"

Blondie opened his file and pulled out the charging documents. "Comes now the State of Washington," he read, "by and through the undersigned Deputy Prosecuting Attorney and alleges that the defendant, Amelia Jenkins, did, in the State of Washington, commit the crime of assault in the first degree as follows: did, with intent to inflict great bodily harm, assault another person with a firearm or other deadly weapon or by any force or means likely to produce great bodily harm, contrary to Revised Code of Washington 9A.36.011(1)(a)."

Stubble shook his head again. "I guess I can see the deadly weapon part, maybe. I mean a car can be a deadly weapon. But how do they think they're going to prove she had the intent to inflict great bodily harm? Wasn't she just trying to drive away?"

"She was," Blondie agreed, "but the cop will say he was standing there and she drove right at him."

"So, the cop will lie," Stubble translated.

Blondie nodded. "Right. He's a cop."

"So, what's the offer?" Stubble asked. "Did you ask for the Assault Four?"

"I did, but it just couldn't come across as serious," Blondie answered. "They're never gonna knock an Assault One all the way down to Assault Four."

"That's part of why they charged it that way," Stubble observed.

"I know."

"So, what's the offer?"

"Assault Two, plus a couple of other felonies to increase her sentencing range," Blondie explained. "Attempting to elude a police vehicle and felony harassment. That gets her to twelve months, and that means she goes to prison instead of doing her time locally."

"Police vehicle?" Stubble laughed. "Weren't they on foot?"

Blondie shrugged. "It's just another felony to give her more points. They want to increase her sentencing range enough to give her a year sentence, so she goes to state prison."

Stubble shook his head. "What is she looking at if she rejects it and goes down at trial?"

"The range will be ninety-three to a hundred and twenty-three months," Blondie answered. "And they'll ask for the high end. Probably get it too."

"So, one year versus ten years," Stubble summarized. "Seems like an easy decision."

Up to that point in the conversation, Talon had remained silent, satisfied to learn what she could about the not-crime that unfolded before her very eyes. What was said next would determine whether she interjected herself into the discussion. She agreed with Stubble: it was an easy decision. The defendant was innocent. You don't plead out an innocent client to a year in prison. You go to trial. But she suspected she wasn't going to agree with Blondie's response.

"Easy peezy, prison squeeze me," Blondie said. "She's taking that twelve-month sentence, if I have to sign her name on the plea form myself."

"That would be a crime and a bar complaint," Talon interrupted. "I hope whoever you hire to defend you cares more about you than you do about your clients."

Blondie's happy grin melted from his face. "I'm sorry. Were we talking to you?"

"You were talking loud enough for everybody to hear you," Talon responded. "Also, I don't really give a fuck if you were talking to me. I heard what you said, and what you said sucks. So, now I'm talking to you."

Blondie pushed away from the table and stood up. He had a boyish face but the body of a man, towering over Talon by several inches. She supposed he was trying to intimidate her. She didn't intimidate that easily.

"Do I know you?" he asked, implying he should if she was important, and he didn't, ergo she wasn't.

"You will," was Talon's reply.

"She must do civil, Mike," Stubble interrupted. "She's all dressed up for court on a Friday morning. The bar association lounge is back by the elevators, if you're looking for the Friday morning donuts your dues pay for."

Talon was a bit disappointed not to be recognized. Then again, she didn't recognize these two hacks either. They had likely started doing felony work about the time she started focusing on *The Tribe v. Yacht Club*. How quickly you're forgotten.

"Do yourself, and us, a favor, and leave the criminal cases to the experts," Blondie advised. "Forget what you weren't meant to overhear anyway, and leave the grownups to work out the really big cases, 'kay?"

Talon wasn't one to forget things. More importantly, she was one to make sure other people didn't forget things, like her fist in their throat. Metaphorically, of course. She wasn't going to jail for assaulting the loser in front of her.

"I'll give you something not to forget, Mike," she answered. "But not quite yet. I'm going to make you wait for it."

She laced the last sentence with a drop of sultriness, to evoke the subtle suggestiveness of the words. Not that she had even the slightest interest in Mike Blondmop. It was just that men, for the most part, were idiots when it came to dealing with attractive women. The slightest hint that they might have a million-in-one chance to score, and their higher thought processes were scrambled by a rush of blood away from the brain. Even if she didn't do anything else, he'd remember her. But she was definitely going to do something else.

She turned on her heel and headed out of The Pit—into the courtroom where she knew Blondie and whichever prosecutor was assigned to the case would have to appear to confirm whether the case was ready to proceed to trial, had reached a resolution, or neither and needed more time for negotiations. It was one of the two main criminal courtrooms that ran all day, every day. One of them did guilty pleas all morning and arraignments all afternoon, giving the prosecutors time to review each morning's reports from the new arrests the night before. The other courtroom, the one Talon walked into, was for the cases between arraignment and sentencing. The judges required the attorneys to check in periodically, lest a case languish forever while prosecutors offered shitty deals and defense attorneys waited for better ones.

The courtroom itself was built for the convenience of the judges and attorneys, and the security needed for defendants to appear in court even while they were being held in jail pending trial. Not so much for the convenience of the defendants themselves, or the public, for that matter.

Presumed innocent, my ass, Talon thought as she nodded

pleasantly to the jail guard standing sentry by the heavy metal door that led to the holding cells behind the courtroom. Inmates were brought over from the jail, held in the cells until their cases were called, then brought into the courtroom, still handcuffed, to stand before the judge while the lawyers talked about them as if they weren't even there. They were then returned to the holding cells until every one of them was done and they could be transported back to the jail *en masse*. Great system. Great for the judges anyway. And the prosecutors. Not so much for the defense attorneys who might want to actually speak to their clients at some point before or after a hearing.

It wasn't great for the public either, even though they had a right to observe all court proceedings. The state constitution's open courtroom provision required all cases to be open to the public at all times. But it didn't say they couldn't put up a glass barrier with a locked door and pipe the proceedings into the sectioned off gallery over tinny speakers. The judge sat at the front of the courtroom, above everyone else. The lawyers whose case was actively being addressed stood before the judge. The lawyers who were waiting to be next sat inside at the edge of the fishbowl with the jail guards. The public could sit on the other side of the locked glass, basically in another room, out of sight and out of mind. Even Talon didn't give much thought to the few dozen people waiting on the other side of the glass to catch a momentary glimpse of their loved ones before they were swallowed again by The System.

She wasn't there for any of them after all. She was there for Blondie.

It took him another fifteen minutes or so to enter the courtroom via the side door to The Pit. Talon passed the time checking her phone and half-listening to the procession of cases parading past the bench. She enjoyed being immersed in the sights and sounds, and even smells, of criminal practice. She felt at home and fully recharged by the time Blondie walked in, and she wished she'd been disappointed when he did so alongside the prosecutor, yukking it up over some lame joke the prosecutor had made, probably at the defendant's expense. Talon hated seeing defense attorneys suck up to prosecutors. She especially hated it when the prosecutor was someone who both knowingly reveled in it and unknowingly hadn't earned that kind of deference. She hated that prosecutor. She hated Eric Quinlan.

They had history. Talon's first case after setting up her own criminal defense practice was against Quinlan. He was unjustifiably arrogant, although Talon supposed that was standard for prosecutors. They won most of their cases, but only because the defendants were usually guilty of something, even if not exactly what they were charged with. Throw in the fact that the cops did all the work and the juries thought of the prosecutors as the heroes of the courtroom, and it was almost a challenge for them to screw up enough to lose. Quinlan carried himself with the full confidence of a mediocre White prosecutor. And Blondmop was just feeding the beast.

"Are there any other matters ready?" the judge called out from the bench. It was Judge Rodney Kalamaka, only recently appointed to the bench to fill a vacancy after one of the oldest judges in the county was forced to finally step down for medical issues. Life took its toll on everyone eventually, and when it did, newbies like Rodney Kalamaka got a foot on the ladder. But it was the bottom rung, and that meant doing scheduling hearings all day, every day, trying to keep the rushing, never-ending river of criminal cases from spilling over the banks.

He was young and still affable, not having been worn down completely by the job yet. His background was family law; that was why they had put him in the criminal rotation first. He could hardly preside over divorce cases if he or his old firm had previously been the lawyer on the case. It would take a while for those conflict cases to settle out over the natural course of time. Plus, there were two added bonuses for the other judges. One, they wouldn't have to do the daily criminal calendar, and two, dealing with an unfamiliar area of the law would humble the new judge, lest he think he really was all that and a bag of chips, just because he'd been selected from a few dozen applicants to take up the empty spot on the Pierce County Superior Court.

"The Jenkins matter is ready, Your Honor," Quinlan seized the opportunity before the door to The Pit had even closed behind them. He nodded to the jail guard, who in turn opened the door to the holding cells and called out, "Jenkins!"

Blondie and Quinlan took their respective spots at the bar in front of Judge Kalamaka as they waited for the defendant to be escorted into the courtroom. When she entered, flanked by a corrections officer, dressed in gray jail scrubs, and handcuffed in front, Talon knew for certain it was the woman she had seen in front of the courthouse that day.

"This is the matter of *The State of Washington versus Amelia Jenkins,*" Quinlan announced the case. "Eric Quinlan on behalf of the State."

"And Michael Wheaton appearing on behalf of the defendant, Your Honor," Blondie put in his appearance. *Wheaton.* Talon decided to hate the name, just on principle.

"All right, then," Judge Kalamaka accepted the case. "How are we proceeding today? Are the parties ready to schedule a trial date?"

Quinlan looked to Wheaton, who knew he was supposed to answer the question. "Uh, no, Your Honor. I believe we have reached a resolution. We are asking the Court to schedule the matter for a change of plea."

"Change of plea?" Jenkins asked her lawyer. "Like, plead guilty?"

Nice. Talon frowned. Wheaton hadn't even talked to his client about the deal before accepting it.

Wheaton raised a hand at Jenkins. "I've got this. We'll talk about the deal before the next hearing."

"A deal?" Jenkins's tone lightened. "Am I getting out?"

Not by a long shot, Talon thought.

But she overheard Wheaton's whispered answer. "Yes. I can explain it all once we're done with court."

'Yes.' Talon was shocked. She understood that it was technically true. Yes, she would be getting out of jail, eventually. But first she would get shipped to state prison for a year. Talon felt confident that's not what Jenkins meant when she asked if she was getting out.

"Will we be doing the sentencing at the same time?" Kalamaka asked. "No need for a pre-sentence report or anything?"

Pre-sentence reports by the county probation department were required on certain offenses, mostly sex offenses, to provide the judge with additional information about the crime and the defendant before settling on a sentence. But a simple fake assault on a cop, with an agreed sentencing recommendation from the prosecution and defense? No need.

"All right then," the judge said. "How about one week from today? Or do the parties need two weeks?"

"One week will be fine," Wheaton assured the judge.

"What's going on?" Talon heard Jenkins whisper, her voice becoming increasingly desperate. It was a strange byproduct of the right to a lawyer that defendants often lost their own voices in the process.

Wheaton didn't even bother to answer. He just put up his hand again to silence her.

But he couldn't silence Talon.

"Your Honor," she called out, standing up from her seat at the edge of the courtroom, "I'm Talon Winter, and—"

"I know who you are, Ms. Winter," Judge Kalamaka interjected. "Are you involved in this case?"

"Not directly, Your Honor," Talon answered, "but I was listening to the proceedings. If this is going to be a guilty plea, might I suggest a Wednesday setting? The bus that transports inmates from the county jail to the state prison system leaves every week on Thursday mornings."

Language could be interesting. The same information could be provided in various ways depending on the audience. If Talon had truly been speaking to the judge, and the lawyers for that matter, she would have just said, 'The chain runs on Thursdays.' They all would have known what that meant. But Amelia Jenkins would not have, and that's who Talon was really speaking to. By spelling it out like that, not only did Jenkins understand, but Wheaton, Quinlan, and Judge Kalamaka all knew she was really speaking to Amelia Jenkins. Not that they could do anything about it.

"Prison?!" Jenkins shrieked. "You said I was getting out!"

"She's not getting out," Quinlan chuckled to himself, but far too loud not to be heard.

Jenkins's head spun toward him, then back to Wheaton. "You lied to me!"

Wheaton raised both of his palms to her. "Now, just calm down, Amelia. I can explain."

If there were two things a woman didn't want to hear from a

man they were, 'Calm down', and, 'I can explain'.

"I am not going to prison!" Jenkins shouted. She reached right between Wheaton's ineffective hands and shoved him squarely in the chest. He stumbled backward, tripped over his own feet, and fell on his ass in front of the judge, God, and everyone. Talon didn't even try to suppress her smile.

The guards were less amused. They jumped on Jenkins and easily wrestled her to the ground. A moment later they were dragging her backward toward the holding cells, even as she continued to shout, "I'm not going to fucking prison! Not for this, you mother fuckers!"

It took a few moments before a semblance of calm began to return to the courtroom. Once that happened, Talon looked up again to the judge. "My apologies, Your Honor. I just couldn't imagine a defense attorney scheduling a guilty plea without first telling their client what the plea bargain was, especially if it involved prison time."

The judge stared down at Talon, but didn't immediately respond. He obviously wasn't buying that. But what could he do about it? He sighed, and returned his mind to the work at hand. "I think perhaps we should wait to schedule that plea hearing until Mr. Wheaton has had a chance to speak more with his client." He lifted his gaze to the rest of the courtroom. "Are there any other matters ready?"

Talon took that as her cue to exit, but before she could quite reach the door to The Pit, Wheaton scurried in front of her.

"Just who do you think you are?" he demanded, still out of breath from being thrown on his ass by a handcuffed woman.

"I'm Talon Winter," she answered, stepping around him to grab the door handle. "I told you you'd learn my name."

CHAPTER 7

"Talon Winter, damn it," she laughed to herself as she stepped out into the late morning sun. Sometimes she really liked her name. Even more so when it popped up on a text from Zack Claymore of Portland. She felt her phone vibrate at the arrival of the text and pulled it out to look at it.

Hi, Talon. Zack here. Curt's friend. Was hoping you might show me one of those great places around town. Are you free tonight?

She smiled. She didn't have plans, but Zack wasn't getting it for free. He'd have to earn it. And a part of her—an admittedly neglected part of her lately—really hoped he would be up to the task. So to speak.

She was going to accept the invitation, but not immediately. It wasn't a game exactly, but she still intended to win. She knew she could wait until the end of the day to agree to meet him. And she knew he'd say yes. She also knew where they would go for dinner. And where they would go afterward.

* * *

Dinner was at *La Mer d'Or*.

Drinks started at 6:30.

The food arrived at 7:30.

Dessert was served at 8:45, and the check was paid by 9:00.

Talon had picked the best place closest to her condo. They were there by 9:15.

Drinks and dinner and dessert were all fine and dandy. You had to eat, and you might as well enjoy it. But the most important purpose of the date was to get the small talk out of the way so that by the time she got Zack the Out-of-Town Firefighter back to her place, she didn't have to waste time talking to him.

"Nice place you've got here," he started to say as they stepped over the threshold.

But Talon put a finger to his lips and shook her head. "Shh," she said. "This isn't about you."

She grabbed him by the shoulders and spun him around, then pushed him backward toward her bedroom. He didn't resist. When they arrived, she shoved him onto the bed and started to take off her shirt and bra. Zack pulled his own shirt over his head, revealing the muscular arms and torso Talon knew were beneath. She pulled him to his feet again and kissed him deeply as she undid his belt. He reached around and unclasped her skirt, which fell to the floor just before his pants did. Underwear followed immediately and Talon grabbed him by those broad shoulders again. She knew how it was going to start and where she needed to position the both of them for it to happen.

She sat down on the edge of the bed, pulling him close. Then she pushed him to his knees and leaned onto her back. He knew what to do. She hoped he also knew how.

He did.

Not perfectly, of course. Not immediately. Everyone was different. Everyone liked different things. There were some things almost everyone liked, of course. The broad-brush things. General categories of activities and positions. But the finer lines were a matter of individual taste. Zack was paying attention to her responses and adjusting accordingly. His mouth was soft but firm, his tongue hot and quick, his hands strong as they held her legs apart. He let go of one leg and slid a single finger inside her, then two, without stopping the work of that hot, quick tongue. She reached down and held his head, pressing it against her, making sure he didn't stop. Not yet. But soon. She wasn't ready for it to end too soon, but he was making it difficult to want to go slow.

Her back arched and her hips ground herself against his mouth and fingers. She released a hand from his hair and caressed her own neck and breasts as the waves inside her grew stronger and faster. Then she grabbed that hair of his and pulled his face away from her, looking down with satisfaction at the glistening on his mouth and chin.

She didn't have to say it, but she did anyway. "Fuck me."

Zack smiled, his perfectly carved chest heaving already at the exertion of pleasing her. He fumbled through his pants on the floor and pulled out his wallet. A moment later he was standing over her, pulling on protection, preparing to carry out her order.

Talon pushed herself back from the edge of the bed and dropped her head onto the pillows piled at the headboard. She was glistening too, matching his face, and she opened her legs to him as he climbed first onto the bed and then onto her.

Talon took a moment to look at the beautiful man perched over her. His strong jawline. His bright eyes. The rippled muscles of the arms on either side of her. And then she closed her eyes to all that as he thrust himself inside her, deep and thick and hard.

She grabbed the back of his head and pulled his face into her neck. She accepted his rhythm and rocked back against it, feeling the length of his body atop her. He was paying attention to her again, adjusting his speed, his depth, his motion in response to her body and her moans. Damn, he was good.

He pushed his chest off of her and locked eyes with her even as they were also still locked together lower. Talon looked into his eyes for several seconds, but it was too much. He wasn't there for her to gaze into his eyes. She pushed his face away and rolled him over onto his back, breaking their connection, but only momentarily as she quickly straddled him and guided him back inside of her.

She could set the pace now, arching upward, closing her eyes. She had an image of that pretty face of his in her mind. She didn't have to actually look at it while she experienced the rest of his body. He grabbed her hips and guided them into a joint rhythm. The penetration was deeper in that position and she leaned forward slightly onto his chest, resting some of her weight on her arms. He reached up and cupped her breasts as he increased the pace of his thrusts. She fell forward and buried her own face into his strong muscular neck. His skin smelled good, helping her to lose herself in the experience of him surrounding her.

They disentangled again, not clearly initiated by either one of them in particular, and Talon perched herself onto her hands and knees at the edge of the bed. Zack rolled off the bed and stepped up behind her. Now she could really forget his face if she wanted. She wasn't sure if she wanted to, she realized, but then lost that thought as he guided himself to her, grabbed her hips and plunged himself inside her again.

Talon fell forward slightly onto her elbows and braced herself against him, her hands grasping the sheets into bunches. She lowered her head onto the mattress as he drove himself home over and over. Eventually, her right hand released the bedsheets and reached between her legs. She was ready to finish.

She was well on her way there when Zack abruptly pulled out and pulled her hand from its work. In one smooth motion, he pushed her forward, laid down next to her, then rolled her over into his arms, replacing her hand with his own. At first, Talon felt annoyed at the interruption, especially because it hadn't always been her experience that her partner could even succeed at the endeavor. But it only took a few moments to allay those concerns. She closed her eyes and leaned back into his embrace, and his efforts.

It didn't take long at all and Talon found herself on the edge of the crest of waves about to wash over her body. Despite herself, she opened her eyes and stared into Zack's as she climaxed, her body arching in his grasp, his eyes strong and kind as she gave herself over to him, even if only for the pleasantly long moments it took for her body to ride out the waves crashing inside her. She smiled at herself and looked away again, satisfied and happy in the moment. Then, before the feeling had completely faded, Zack climbed back on top of and inside her.

Talon wrapped her arms around his back and held on tight as he extended her pleasure and brought his own to completion. He let out a deep grunt as he finished, then collapsed most of his weight onto her, their bodies sweaty and spent and entwined.

Talon savored the moment, but only for a moment. Then she pushed him off of her and sat up on the edge of the bed.

"I'm going to shower," she announced. "You can wait here."

CHAPTER 8

Sometimes you just needed a good lay. And it was a very good lay. The glow lasted all weekend. The best part was that Zack didn't text her even once afterward. No clingy, needy guy, thinking he was in love with her just because they boned and the sex was good. She recalled the look in his eyes when they had both finished. Satisfaction, admiration, confidence.

Yep, she told herself, the best part was that he didn't text all weekend. She parked her car outside her office, ready to start another week, and checked her phone one last time. Nope, no texts.

Good, she assured herself. *Good.*

But texts or no texts, she was still glowing as she walked into the lobby of her office building and was almost immediately pounced on by the woman seated in the chair nearest the door.

"That's her!" the woman shouted. "That's you. You're that lawyer we saw in court on Friday. You're that Talon Winter."

She was, in fact, that Talon Winter. She was also confused. But she wasn't one to stay confused.

"That's me," she acknowledged. "Who are you? And why are you looking for me?"

The woman smiled broadly and looked back at a man still

seated where the woman had leapt from. "This is her," she called back. "I told you it was her. There's no way there's two Talon Winters in this town."

"I doubt there are two Talon Winters in the entire world," Talon added. "What can I do for you?"

That was the same question she had already asked—'Why are you looking for me?—but it a more pleasant construction. She surmised from the woman's excitement and the man's knowing grin that they were fans, not stalkers or former opponents.

"We need your help," the woman said. "My sister needs your help. She was the one in court with you on Friday. She was the one whose lawyer wants to send her to prison."

"Amelia?" Talon recalled the woman's name. "Amelia Jenkins?"

"See?" the woman spun around again to her companion. "I told you she'd remember Amelia. I told you she would help us."

Talon raised her hands at that. "Whoa. Let's slow down a minute. I'm not sure I can necessarily help. Amelia already has an attorney."

The woman's broad smile dropped. "She doesn't want that lawyer. She wants you."

"Well, you think she might want me," Talon replied, "but it's not your decision. It's hers."

"She's the one who sent us," the woman explained. She pointed at the man again, who reached back and pulled out his wallet. "And we have a credit card."

"Oh, well, in that case," Talon grinned, "yes, I believe I can help Amelia."

* * *

Talon escorted them to her office on the third floor and used the elevator ride to get the small talk out of the way. The woman's name was Jennifer Bourdain. The man was her husband, Hank. Amelia Jenkins was her younger sister. They all lived in Tacoma. Jennifer was a school teacher. Hank worked for the power company. Amelia was a medical technician, unmarried, no kids. Jennifer had always watched out for Amelia and things weren't about to change now that she was really in trouble.

When they reached Talon's office, she invited the Bourdains to sit opposite her across her desk, then began the meeting in earnest.

"Tell me what you know about Amelia's case," she directed, "and why she wants to hire me."

"We know she's being railroaded for something she didn't do," Jennifer said, "because she dared to try to hold the cops accountable for police brutality."

Talon nodded. That sounded about right. It hadn't quite reached the level of brutality, she recalled, but it was certainly headed in that direction. Amelia's actions had stopped that, although at a personal cost.

"And why does she want to hire me?" Talon prompted.

"Because of what you did when her current lawyer tried to trick her into pleading guilty and going to prison," Jennifer answered. She gestured to her husband. "We were there too, in the gallery. We saw it all. You were awesome. You made sure she knew what was happening to her even if her own lawyer wouldn't tell her."

Hank grinned. "Very sneaky," he admired.

Talon shrugged. "I'm not sure about that," she demurred.

"No," Hank replied. "It's a good thing. They're being shady. We need someone who can be shady too. You can't win the game if you play by different rules."

Talon smiled back, but avoided confirming the metaphor.

She wasn't going to play by the cops' rules either. She had her own rules, thank you very much.

"How's Amelia doing?" she asked instead. Showing a little human concern could seal the deal, and despite having more than enough work to do—Tribe, meet Yacht Club—she felt a personal draw to Amelia's case. It wasn't every day she witnessed firsthand the injustice she was fighting against.

Jennifer smiled at the question. She probably hadn't expected anything as humane as that. It was a business transaction, after all. But it was going to end up being more than that, Talon knew. It would have to be, if they were going to win.

"She's hanging in there," Jennifer assured.

"Barely," Hank qualified. "I don't know how much more she can take. It's hard enough for anybody to be in jail, but when you're innocent? That makes everything a hundred times worse."

Talon nodded. There were plenty of inmates who knew they were guilty and were just hoping their lawyers could get them a deal and cut some time off their sentences. That wasn't what Amelia was looking for. Blondie had gotten her that. And now Jennifer and Hank Bourdain were in her office.

"I should go visit her," Talon offered. She took a moment to pull up her calendar on her phone. "In fact, I have time this morning."

"Don't you want to talk about money first?" Jennifer asked. "We haven't even hired you yet, technically."

Talon knew not to smile too broadly at that. Just enough to acknowledge the comment. She pulled open her desk drawer and extracted a blank copy of her standard fee agreement.

"Well, then," she said, "let's get that out of the way. My retainer is due in full, up front, and it's non-refundable."

Jennifer swallowed hard and looked to her husband, who

just shrugged and gestured back to Talon.

"That's standard in criminal cases, I assure you," Talon said. She wrote the fee amount on the blank line in paragraph one of the contract. It wasn't going to be cheap to defend a Class A felony, especially one allegedly committed against a cop.. "But I accept all major credit cards."

Jennifer nodded, then looked again to her husband for confirmation. He gave it by pulling out his wallet and extracting one of those credit cards.

"Excellent," Talon acknowledged. "As soon as we get this out of the way, I'll head over to the jail and introduce Amelia to her new lawyer."

CHAPTER 9

Pierce County had two jails. Business was booming. The 'Old Jail' was physically connected to that cardboard-box structure of the County-City Building. In fact, it was at that corner of the block, right in front of the Old Jail, that Amelia Jenkins had 'assaulted' the cop who ran in front of her car. The 'New Jail', on the other hand, was built in the parking lot behind the County-City Building. For a while after it was built, it was the 'Empty Jail' because, while the county government had authorized its construction, they didn't want to pay union scale to the additional corrections officers they would need to guard the inmates they wanted to house there. It stood empty for almost a year, a testament to poor planning and misplaced frugality. Eventually, though, the guards got their pay and the New Jail got its inmates, including Amelia Jenkins.

Amelia's cell was on the second floor. From the outside, the New Jail looked like it had windows, but they were actually just glass blocks imbedded in the brick wall to give the illusion of windows. There was no natural light inside, not even in the small attorney-client conference room Talon was escorted to for her meeting with her new client. It was the same cinderblock walls and fluorescent lights as the Old Jail. The same lingering smell of institutionalized food and industrial solvent. The same sense of despair and desperation. Luckily, Talon could light up the place on her own. She was, after all, a ray of fucking sunshine.

The only difference between the Old Jail and the New Jail, at least the only one relevant to her client meeting, was the physical layout of the conference room. In the Old Jail, they were both in the same room with a guard standing watch outside the door. In the New Jail, they were separated by a partition of plexiglass, with an opening at the bottom barely big enough to slide two pieces of paper under, and a circle of drilled holes at face level meant to allow for conversation. It did, but only barely, and only if they both leaned forward and shouted a bit. Talon was not a fan. She sat in her chair, arms crossed, and waited for the arrival of Amelia Jenkins.

When the door on the other side of the partition clanked open, Talon immediately adjusted her presentation. Surly and irritated was all fine and good for the guards that escorted her to the supposedly private conference room you had to shout in, but it wouldn't do for winning over a potential new client. And despite that hefty charge on Hank Bourdain's credit card and the boilerplate phrase 'non-refundable fee, earned upon receipt' in her fee agreement, Talon knew she wouldn't really be able to keep the money if the defendant herself took one look at Talon, dropped her head to the side, and uttered, 'Nope.' Talon didn't want to lose that fee. More importantly, she didn't want to lose that client.

She stood up and offered a crisp nod. "Good morning, Ms. Jenkins. My name is Talon Winter. Your sister hired me to be your attorney."

Amelia looked about as bad as she had at court the previous Friday. Just worn out. People think jail is scary, but mostly it's boring, and tiring. It's not a natural or comfortable way to live. That wears on a person. Amelia had been in custody since the incident. No wonder she panicked at the thought of months more in state prison.

"I know who you are," Amelia responded. She nodded toward the door behind her and what lay beyond. "A bunch of people in here know who you are. They say you're good."

"They're right," Talon confirmed. It wasn't being cocky if it was true. "I'm even better than that."

"I hope so," Amelia replied. She pulled out her chair and sat down. Talon followed suit. The circle of drilled holes encircled Amelia's nose and mouth. "Anybody would be better than that Wheaton asshole. He was gonna sell me up the river. Thank God you were there to make sure I knew what was going on."

Talon wasn't sure God had anything to do with it. If He actually cared about the things that happened in the criminal justice system, and what people did to get themselves into the criminal justice system, none of that would happen in the first place, and she'd have to find honest work.

"Just watching out for a fellow cop-hater," Talon replied. "You must really hate them if you tried to First Degree Assault one of them."

"I didn't try to assault anyone," Amelia called out. "I was trying to get away. I shouldn't have gotten involved in the first place. I'm an idiot."

But Talon shook her head. "No. You're a hero."

"A hero?" Amelia laughed. "No. Maybe you are, defending people from bogus charges. But me? No, I'm just somebody who made a bad decision and now I'm paying for it."

"You made the right decision," Talon returned. "You saw an injustice and you did something to stop it. That's why they're coming after you. That's why you're a hero."

Amelia shook her head and gazed downward. "I'm sorry, but I just can't believe that."

"It doesn't matter if you believe it," Talon explained, "so long as the jury does."

Amelia raised her face again and smiled at her new advocate. "I knew I was right to hire you."

CHAPTER 10

Whoever said you shouldn't mix work with pleasure either didn't have a fun job or had too many options in the pleasure department. Probably both. Talon, on the other hand, had a kick-ass job. And her options for pleasure remained high as Zack was still in town and did in fact text her again after waiting the exact right amount of time to do so.

I'd love to see you again, he texted.

She wanted to fuck him again too.

She told him to dress like he was going to dinner at a yacht club. He didn't realize she meant it literally. But he'd aced the assignment. Open-collared shirt under a navy blazer, nice pants, and brown loafers. She wouldn't mind being seen with him. She just hoped she wouldn't be noticed.

"Wait," Zack said as Talon pulled into the parking lot next to the Commencement Bay Yacht Club, "we're really going to a yacht club for dinner?"

Talon grinned. "Why not?"

"Do you own a boat?" he asked.

"No," she answered, "but I'm looking at acquiring some waterfront property. For a client, I mean."

"Ah." Zack nodded as Talon pulled into a parking stall. "You're not telling me everything, are you?"

"Do you want to know everything?" Talon asked. "Or do you want to be treated to a luxury meal with a view of the bay?" She glanced down at her own appropriately dressy ensemble. "And of me?"

Zack couldn't argue with that. At the very least, he was smart enough not to. "I know everything I need to know. Let's enjoy a dinner with the most beautiful scenery in the Northwest."

Talon appreciated how he left it open whether he meant the water or her. Maybe both. Definitely both. She reached over and cupped a hand on his cheek. "Smart boy."

She turned off the car and stepped out into the evening air. The smell of the water mixed pleasantly with the cooking inside the club's restaurant. Regardless of the success of her reconnaissance mission, she was confident they were going to enjoy a delicious meal. Maybe the Tribe could keep the restaurant after they wrested their land back.

Zack followed her out of the car and across the lot toward the entrance. He knew not to try putting his arm around her. That was never as romantic as it seemed. It was mostly just awkward and threw off both people's gait.

"Oh, by the way," Talon informed him as they reached the door, "the reservation is under 'Claymore'."

"You made the reservation in my name?" he asked. "Why?"

"I wanted you to feel involved," she answered without looking at him.

"You called me, you picked what we're doing, you picked the place, you told me what to wear," Zack recounted, "but you want me to feel involved?"

"Did it work?" she grinned sidelong at him.

"Not really, no," Zack answered as he pulled the door open for her, "but I'm okay with it. 'Claymore, party of two.' Has a nice ring to it, don't you think?"

Uh-oh. Talon frowned. He wasn't going there, was he? Not that fast. There was no way they were anywhere close to talking about 'Talon Claymore, Attorney at Law.'

"Just make sure we get a good table, Claymore," she growled at him. "I doubt I'll be coming back here anytime soon."

As Zack approached the hostess stand to secure that good table, Talon hung back to examine whatever might be hanging on the wall nearest her. Not surprisingly, it was a series of photographs of old White men standing in front of large boats holding silly trophies. Brass plaques embedded in the matting listed the year, competition, and place finished. The one directly in front of her was for finishing in '11th Place' in some 'Regalia' run in '1977'. In fact, all of the photos on that particular lobby wall were from the 1970s, but a glance around the restaurant confirmed the rest of the decades were represented throughout the interior. That was a lot of trophy/boat/old White guy photos. Talon guessed the Association of Colonizer Yacht Clubs made sure everyone got a trophy, if only to ensure pretentious décor for all of their members' restaurants.

"Claymore, table for two," Zack interrupted her sour thoughts. "Right this way."

He gestured to the hostess who in turn gestured toward the seating area and their waiting table. It was a cozy little thing, right up against the windows, with a white tablecloth, a single votive candle, and a view of the water over the tops of the boats moored at the club. Talon directed Zack into one of the chairs, so she could have the other one—the one with the additional view of the interior of the restaurant, including the door to the kitchen and back offices.

"This is very nice," Zack admired the view. "I'd say we

don't have anything like this back in Portland, but we probably do. I just don't spend a lot of time at yacht clubs."

"Yeah, me neither," Talon admitted. She opened one of the menus. "I wonder if the food is any good."

Zack gazed around again. "It looks like it should be."

Talon didn't respond. She was already busy watching the comings and goings of the restaurant staff. She wasn't really sure what she was looking for, or why she had wanted to come there. Part of it was just basic investigation. You always go to the scene of the crime. There just isn't usually a luxury restaurant built on top of it. She had gotten used to crime scene tape and blood stains. She thought she preferred it to what she was witnessing then.

She returned her gaze to her dining companion, whom she found looking expectantly at her. He must have said something she didn't listen to.

"Sorry, did you say something?" she asked.

"I just asked if anything looked good," Zack answered. "Stupid small talk. I'm not very good at it."

"Yeah, me either," Talon admitted. "It's a waste of time and energy."

"Agreed," Zack said. "So, are we going to sit in silence or are you going to tell me why we're really at this place neither of us would ever normally go to?"

Talon frowned at him, but she couldn't hold the expression. She appreciated his insightfulness. And she didn't want to spend the next hour talking about the weather or sports or the latest show everyone was watching.

"Your choice," she replied. "I can do awkward silence."

"I don't doubt that," Zack chuckled, "but let's do the other thing. I bet it's way more interesting. Are you a secret agent or spy or something? Is some evil mastermind about to walk in wearing a monocle and stroking a cat?"

"Seriously?" Talon's frown returned. "You can do better than that."

Zack accepted the challenge with a nod. "Ok, that's fair. Let me see. You're a lawyer. You mostly defend people charged with serious crimes. This has something to do with your work. Am I getting warm?"

"That's room temperature at best," Talon chided. "If this isn't the kind of place I would come to in my personal life, that pretty much just leaves work. Not impressive, Claymore. Not impressive at all."

Zack frowned and glanced around again. "This doesn't feel like the kind of place where a serious crime would happen."

Talon nodded. "Sometimes that's a sign of the most serious crimes."

"So, it is a criminal case?" Zack asked.

"I didn't say that," Talon answered.

"You didn't not say that," Zack pointed out.

"Maybe we should try that awkward silence after all," Talon suggested. "It would probably be better than this awkward conversation."

Zack nodded and looked out at the water. "Or we could stop playing twenty questions and you could just tell me what's going on. I'm pretty sure I'll find it entertaining. I might even be able to help. I'm no Curt Fairchild, Private Investigator, but—"

"You can say that again," Talon interrupted, but then regretted it. She had meant it as a dig against Curt, but Zack's fallen expression suggested he had understood it the other way around.

The date was going great already.

Talon took a deep breath. She didn't hate honesty. In fact, she preferred it. But candor was another thing. She liked keeping her cards close to her chest. It went against her nature to divulge information she didn't have to. That was why she was such a good lawyer. But it might also have contributed to why she was not, historically, a terribly successful girlfriend.

"That was a compliment," she started. "Curt is fine. He's a colleague and, I'm willing to admit, a friend. But you shouldn't think he has anything you don't have. Not anything I would be interested in anyway. There's a reason you're here and not him. I can't explain it exactly, but it's real, and I suspect you can understand that. At least, you can, if you're who I think you are."

She had managed to obfuscate a lot of her feelings in that opening salvo of words, but peering out behind them was the truth about how she felt about Curt, and more importantly, how she felt about Zack, at least in that moment.

"Now, as to why we're here," Talon continued, "you're correct. It has to do with my job. But it's not a criminal case. It's a civil case. I'm one of the lawyers on a lawsuit trying to get back the land this yacht club is built on."

"Get back?" Zack cocked his head.

"This land belongs to the Puyallup Tribe of Indians," Talon explained. "Or at least it should. Hence the lawsuit."

Zack narrowed his eyes in thought. "So, you want to see if the restaurant is worth taking over?" he ventured.

Maybe he wasn't better than Curt. She rolled her eyes and sighed.

"That was a joke," Zack added quickly. "I should make that clear. So, right, reconnaissance of some sort or another. Makes sense. The scene of the crime and all that."

He got it after all. Good.

"Anything in particular we should be on the lookout for?" Zack continued. "I'm no lawyer, so I probably wouldn't be able to see the connection between your lawsuit and whatever might be going on here."

Talon wasn't sure either. She was just hoping she might know it when she saw it. They both glanced around the place. Then Talon saw it and knew it.

She could hardly miss it, in fact. It was Peter Grainsley, all 10 feet and 800 pounds of him, filling the entirety of the doorway to the dining room. Talon quickly turned away, suddenly very interested in whatever was on the other side of the window. She pulled her hair forward to cover her face and hoped Grainsley hadn't seen her.

"Are you okay?" Zack asked. "What's wrong?"

It wasn't that Talon was afraid to run into Grainsley. She had handled him just fine at their last meeting and she had every intention of doing so again in every future encounter, up to and including the trial. But if he saw her, and recognized her, the restaurant would be alerted to her presence. and her plans, whatever those might be, would be ruined.

"See that huge guy by the entrance?" Talon whispered.

Zack took a moment to look. "Yeah. He's kind of hard to miss."

"Tell me when he's seated."

"Who is he?"

"Opposing counsel on that lawsuit," Talon explained. "He'll recognize me. I was hoping to be incognito tonight."

"Ah, so you are a spy," Zack teased. "At least tonight."

"I'm a lot of things," Talon answered, "every night. Now shut up and tell me when he's seated."

"Which one?" Zack asked.

"Which thing am I every night?" Talon sought to clarify.

"No, not that," Zack answered. "Although I will admit my

interest is piqued. But no, do you want me to tell you he's seated now, or do you want me to shut up. I can't do both, I don't think."

"Is he seated?"

"Yes."

"Where?'

"Directly behind you."

"Fuck."

"But like four tables away."

"Oh, okay."

"And facing away from you."

Talon exhaled. That was a relief.

"Who is he sitting with?"

Zack peered over her shoulder. "Some old White guy."

"Everyone in here is an old White guy."

"I'm not," Zack protested.

"You will be," Talon pointed out.

Zack frowned but could hardly argue. "Well, you aren't."

"That's why I'm so noticeable."

Zack nodded. "I see your point."

"So, old White guy," Talon repeated, "Anything else?"

"Um," more squinting past her, "bald?"

Talon rolled her eyes. "Ugh. That's like part of being an old White guy."

"Not always," Zack protested. "My grandpa had a full head of hair right up until he passed away."

"Are we really going to have this discussion right now?" Talon hissed.

"I'm just saying."

"Stop saying," Talon replied. "Stop describing. Just take a picture."

"With my phone?"

Another eye roll. "No. Go out to the car and get my old-timey photograph-o-matic with the huge lens and the powder flash."

"You know, Talon," Zack took a moment to say, "you get kind of mean when you're stressed."

"I'm kind of mean all of the time, Zack," Talon returned. "Now take a damn picture, but make sure it doesn't look like you're taking a picture."

"You know that's not possible, right?"

"I know you're pretty good with your hands and doing things that most people can't do," she encouraged him. "Do this right and maybe we can get out of here and you can do some more of those other things too."

Zack smiled. "That's the real reason you asked me out to dinner, isn't it?"

"It's not not one of the reasons," Talon agreed. "Now hurry up."

Zack pulled his phone out of his pocket and held it close to his chest, aiming it just past Talon's body.

"Wait!" she whispered.

"What?" Zack asked.

"It's not going to make a camera shutter click noise, is it?"

"It's on silent," Zack assured her. "Who doesn't have their phone on silent?"

"Probably Curt," Talon guessed.

"But, as previously established, I'm not Curt," Zack replied.

Talon was again glad for that. "Go ahead then."

A few silent moments later, Zack pulled his phone down and announced, "Done. So, do you want to order an appetizer?"

"Are you serious?" Talon hissed. "We're leaving."

She stood up, keeping her back to Grainsley and whoever he

was having dinner with, and positioned herself for a hurried exit.

"Can we grab something to eat somewhere else?" Zack asked. He came around to block the view of her from the other table as they walked out together.

"After," Talon told him.

"After?" he asked. "After what?"

They had reached the lobby and the exit. Talon stood up fully again and pushed open the door to the parking lot. "After," she repeated with a grin. "I told you there was more than one reason I wanted to see you tonight."

CHAPTER 11

It was one thing to have a gourmet meal and let it settle over a nightcap before heading home to finish off the evening. It was another to grab a burger and eat in the car just before that finishing off. Talon wasn't one to finish off on a full stomach. Zack wasn't one to argue. He also wasn't one to disappoint, and as they enjoyed teriyaki delivery in their robes, Talon found herself growing both anxious and bemused at how much she was enjoying the company of Zachary Claymore of Portland.

In fact, the following Monday morning found her musing about how the drive from Tacoma to Portland was only about three hours as she made her way to the offices of Smerk+Nordblum for her periodic status conference regarding the yacht club litigation. But her pleasantly distracting, if somewhat embarrassing, ruminations were cut unceremoniously short upon entry into the conference room.

"What the hell were you thinking?" Smerk demanded.

Talon considered for a moment. "The drive to Portland?" she ventured.

"What? No, not what are you thinking about right now," Smerk huffed. "Last Friday. At the yacht club. Why did you go to the yacht club without telling me?"

Talon narrowed her eyes at him. "Because I went with someone else," she explained. "Why would I tell you about my social life?"

"Because your so-called social life is impacting my professional life," Smerk whined. He picked a document up off the table and shook it at her. "Grainsley just filed this motion to dismiss our lawsuit. He's claiming you snuck into the restaurant at the yacht club in order to eavesdrop on privileged communications with his client."

Talon held up a finger. "First of all, I didn't sneak in. We had reservations and walked in the front door. Second, he was like four tables away. I couldn't hear a thing."

Smerk grabbed his head. "Oh my God! It's true. You really were there. The case is going to be dismissed. I knew we never should have brought you on board. I knew we never should have trusted someone outside the firm. You don't care. You don't care at all!"

"Ok, now just hold on a second, Jason." Talon was losing her patience with his dramatics. "I care about this case at least as much as you do. For you, it's business. For me, it's personal. That's why I went to the yacht club. Because I care. Because I want to win this case and will do whatever it takes to gain an advantage."

"Like eavesdrop on opposing counsel?"

Talon's expression hardened. "I already told you. I did not eavesdrop. Watch yourself, Jason. Do not insinuate I'm a liar."

Smerk obviously wanted to argue the point, but wisely elected not to respond.

"Did he give us the name of whoever he was meeting with?" Talon asked.

"His dinner companion?"

"No, the fucking waiter," Talon grumbled. "Yes, his dinner companion. Did he name him?"

Smerk hesitated as he tried to remember. "Uh, no. No, he just said 'a representative of the client'. But I mean, that makes sense, right? The client is a corporation. He could hardly have dinner with a legally crafted entity."

Talon was actually glad to hear that the dinner guest remained a mystery. Grainsley really was sweating it. "Don't get your suspenders in a bunch, Jason," she told him. "I'll handle this."

"But that's just it, Talon." He said her name like a schoolyard taunt. "We shouldn't have to deal with it. There are enough challenges to this case, especially after you accelerated the trial to a date we can't possibly be ready by. We don't need extra hurdles. It's a waste of time, which means it's a waste of our client's money. Have you thought about how much this is going to cost the Tribe? Your tribe?"

She had not thought of that, although in fairness, she had only just learned about the motion. She would have gotten to that part, eventually.

"So, we don't bill them for my time," she suggested. "My mistake, my time."

"A-ha! So, you admit it was a mistake," Smerk accused.

"I don't admit anything," Talon answered, "ever." She snatched the motion out of Smerk's hand. "I will handle this. And when I'm finished, they will regret ever having filed it."

Smerk crossed his arms. "I doubt that," he sniffed.

But Talon didn't. She had been wondering who she should use her one deposition on. Grainsley's overreaction let her know. Whoever that old White guy on Zack's phone was, he was important. Important enough to have dinner with, important enough to throw a legal hissy fit over being seen with, and important enough not to name in the motion to dismiss. Grainsley knew Talon couldn't possibly have heard what they were talking about. That meant merely seeing them together was the real danger.

She loved being someone else's danger.

CHAPTER 12

Talon had gotten under Grainsley's skin. That was an accomplishment in itself. He had tipped his hand, and she would make him pay. But first, she needed to tip her own hand, because she had been paid. It was time to formally take over the Amelia Jenkins case. And what better time and place than in front of everyone just as Michael 'Blondie' Wheaton thought he was going to succeed in selling *her* client up the river.

Talon returned to The Pit and the criminal presiding courtroom on the other side of it. Guilty pleas all morning, every morning. Wednesday because the chain ran on Thursdays. So, on Wednesday at 8:55 a.m. she was seated at the edge of the courtroom, Notice of Substitution of Counsel in hand, and a song in her heart.

There were several other attorneys already there as well, each focused on their own corner of the Misery Industrial Complex that employed them all. Wheaton wasn't there yet, but that hardly surprised Talon. He seemed like the sort of corner-cutting slacker who was probably late for everything. She was going to enjoy showing him up.

At 9:00 a.m., the judge took the bench. It was Kalamaka

again. He was going to be stuck in presiding for a while. At least he still had a smile on his face. Then again, the day had just begun. Quinlan arrived at 9:01, his eyes darting around the courtroom. He was likely searching for Wheaton, but instead saw Talon. She smiled at him. He didn't smile back. Instead, he took up a position standing on the opposite side of the courtroom, eyes locked on the door from The Pit. Finally, at 9:16, Wheaton arrived, all smiles, his tie already loosened like it was 4:45 on a Friday. He didn't bother looking around the courtroom, so he didn't seem to notice Talon. Instead he walked straight to Quinlan and whispered something in his ear. Whatever it was, Quinlan was clearly not pleased about it. That made Talon happy.

"Is the matter of *State v. Jenkins* ready?" Judge Kalamaka asked. "I see both counsel are here now, and we have a busy calendar this morning."

"Well, I'm not sure, Your Honor," Quinlan started, but Wheaton cut him off.

"We can call the case, Your Honor," he said. "We may need to address a preliminary matter before proceeding with the plea."

Kalamaka frowned at that, but acceded. He nodded to the guard at the door to the holding cells, and a few moments later, after a shout of "Jenkins!", Amelia stepped into the courtroom, looking a combination of confused and annoyed. Talon knew that feeling well. At least the annoyed part.

Amelia also scanned the courtroom and quickly observed Talon. She shrugged askance at Talon, and Talon replied with a confident nod, then stood up, ready to speak at the proper moment.

"This is the matter of *The State of Washington versus Amelia Jenkins*," Quinlan announced the case. "It is scheduled this morning for a change of plea to amended charges of assault in the second degree, attempting to elude a pursuing police vehicle, and felony harassment."

"Are the parties ready to proceed?" Judge Kalamaka asked.

"The defense isn't quite ready this morning, Your Honor," Wheaton started to explain.

"The defense won't ever be ready, Your Honor," Talon interjected. "Ms. Jenkins will not be pleading guilty to anything. She is innocent and will be vindicated at trial."

Very dramatic. And a little irritating to everyone but her. And hopefully her client, who did appear relieved at Talon finally saying something, and especially that.

"Ms. Winter," the judge greeted her, "do you have something to say about this case? Again," he added.

"I do, Your Honor," Talon confirmed, "and not simply as a friend of the Court this time."

She stepped forward and handed copies of her Notice of Substitution to Wheaton, Quinlan, and Kalamaka's bailiff. "I have been hired by Ms. Jenkins to take over her case. My first action as her attorney of record will be to strike this plea and ask the Court to schedule the matter for trial."

Kalamaka accepted the notice from his bailiff and inspected it briefly before looking down to the other two lawyers. "Any objection to the substitution?"

Wheaton threw his hands up. "Not from me, Your Honor. If Ms. Jenkins thinks she can get better representation from her new lawyer, I am more than happy to hand it off."

Kalamaka nodded and looked to the prosecutor. "Mr. Quinlan?"

Quinlan wasn't quite shaking with anger, but he was twitching a bit. "This is unexpected, Your Honor, and frankly, more than a little frustrating. Mr. Wheaton and I had the case worked out. I haven't been preparing the case for trial because I expected it to be a plea. Now, I'll need to subpoena witnesses and prepare exhibits and all of the other things one needs to do to get ready for trial."

You mean, do your job, Talon thought.

Kalamaka seemed to share her sentiment. "Understood, Mr. Quinlan," he said, "but I'm sure you're up to the task. I will allow the substitution. Mr. Wheaton, you are removed from the case. Ms. Winter, you are now the attorney of record for Ms. Jenkins. Do you need a few minutes to speak with Mr. Quinlan about scheduling?"

"I doubt that would be fruitful, Your Honor," Talon answered. "We're ready to select a trial date."

Generally speaking, the criminal court rules required a trial to commence within 60 days of the arraignment, if the defendant was, like Amelia Jenkins, held in custody in lieu of bail. A defendant could partially waive that right and extend the deadline, but Quinlan hadn't sought any such waiver, even though Wheaton surely would have given it to him, because Quinlan thought the case would resolve well within those 60 days. As it stood, Quinlan had burned up over half of those 60 days expecting the case to resolve. The only thing that would help him was that the same court rules dictated that the 60-day period started over if a new attorney came on board. The only thing, because Talon sure as hell wasn't going to help him any.

"Is your client willing to waive her right to a speedy trial," Judge Kalamaka asked, "to give you time to get familiar with the case, Ms. Winter?"

"I'm already completely familiar with the case, Your Honor," Talon answered without getting into the details of exactly where she was standing that day in front of the courthouse, "so, no, we will not be waiving speedy trial. I would suggest the Court set the trial date sooner rather than later, although if the Court wishes to set it outside the time period required, I will be happy to have the case dismissed for violation of my client's right to a speedy trial."

"Ok, just slow down there, Ms. Winter." Judge Kalamaka raised a hand to her. "We will be sure not to violate your client's constitutional rights. Mr. Quinlan, do you have anything to say regarding the matter of a trial date?"

Quinlan shrugged up at the judge. "Your Honor," he began to complain, but he didn't have anything to follow it up with. Quinlan could hardly change the court rules, and Talon was right that the remedy for a trial outside of the speedy trial period would be dismissal, regardless of whether she committed the crimes charged. Which, by the way, she did not.

"All right then," Kalamaka announced. "The plea is stricken and the case will proceed to trial. I will schedule a readiness hearing in forty-five days. The parties will return to the courtroom at one o'clock in the afternoon to confirm the case is ready for trial and receive the assignment of judge and courtroom."

Although it would have been nice to know from the start which judge would preside over the trial, there were too many cases in Pierce County to be able to know it that far in advance. Every judge assigned to a trial rotation presided over trial after trial, sometimes selecting the next jury in the main courtroom while the last jury was still deliberating in the jury room. But the fluid and unpredictable nature of trial work made it impossible to predict for certain when any given case would end. If they expected Judge So-And-So to finish her trial on Monday, that was a guarantee it wouldn't finish until Friday. And if Judge What's-His-Name wasn't supposed to be done with his trial for at least a month, it would settle the next day. Talon would just have to come back in 45 days and hope they got a good judge. She already knew the prosecutor sucked.

The only problem was that Amelia's case was now

scheduled to start right before the trial on *Tribe v. Yacht Club*. She couldn't try both cases at once, but she wasn't going to ask Amelia to waive her constitutional rights because of a calendaring challenge.

"Can we talk for a minute?" Amelia interrupted Talon's thoughts as the guard grabbed ahold of her arm to escort her back to her cell.

It was difficult to talk to a client who was in the courtroom holding cells. They couldn't talk confidentially in the courtroom, and the guards would make everyone wait until it was 'secure' to allow a meeting, which was usually after all of the other cases were heard. Even then, half the time, the guards would just take the inmates back to their normal cells without allowing the meeting or bothering to tell the waiting attorneys. Talon didn't want to spend three hours twiddling her thumbs hoping she might get to talk with Amelia for five minutes before the guards insisted she return to the main jail.

"I'll come visit this afternoon," Talon assured her. "I need to deal with a scheduling issue first."

CHAPTER 13

Talon returned to her office and plopped down in her desk chair to ruminate on how to get out of her current dilemma without either of her clients thinking they were second fiddle. It wasn't just that such an impression could damage the attorney-client relationship. It was that it wouldn't be true. Amelia Jenkins was an innocent woman unjustly facing a decade in prison. The Puyallup Tribe of Indians deserved their land back—really, just the smallest portion of their land, but it could be a start. Both were important and both mattered to Talon. That meant she had to a find a solution. She had to.

She stood up again and walked over to her window with the view of Commencement Bay. There was something about gazing at bodies of water that helped stimulate the problem-solving area of the brain. At least, that's what she was hoping. She just needed a few minutes of peaceful reflection and the solution would come to her as a wave on the ocean.

"Penny for your thoughts." Curt's voice sliced through her office, and her tranquility.

"My thoughts cost a lot more than a penny," Talon replied. The friendly thing to do would have been to turn around and engage in further conversation. She did neither.

"Right, well, anyway," Curt said after a moment. "I saw you were in the office and just wanted to stop by and say hi. See if maybe you wanted to grab lunch or something, if you have time."

Talon had the time, but she didn't have the patience. Not right then anyway. The only thing worse than trying to think of a solution to a difficult problem was trying to think of a solution to a difficult problem while someone kept interrupting. But she did go ahead and turn around.

"Not today, Curt," she declined the invitation. "I've got a lot on my plate. I don't think I'd be very good company."

But Curt just smiled. "I could be good enough company for us both."

Talon nodded. "That's what I'm afraid of."

Curt cocked his head at her, a confused expression on his handsome face. She had to admit, she would probably miss him if he wasn't around. Just not right then.

"I need time to think, Curt. That's all," she explained. "I can't do that if we're talking about last night's sportsball game or whatever."

"Maybe I can help," he offered.

He was earnest, she'd give him that. But not much more. "Thanks, Curt. But no thanks."

Curt took a few moments to just nod in contemplation. Then, he shrugged and asked, "How's the case going?"

Talon scoffed. "Which one?"

Then she realized what he was doing. "Thanks, Curt. But seriously. I just need to be alone so I can think."

"Okay," he finally agreed. "I'll be in my office if you need anything."

I won't, she thought as he stepped into the hallway.

"Oh, by the way," he yelled back to her from the corridor. "There are flowers for you at the front desk. I think they might be from Zack."

What?! she thought. "What?" she called out.

"Flowers from Zack," Curt repeated, his voice ever more distant. "Probably to say goodbye. He left for Portland this morning."

"Without saying goodbye?" she asked aloud. Then, a bit shocked at herself, she added in a mumble, "Which is fine. It's not like it was serious. Just some fun while it lasted."

Still, after a pause of a respectable amount of time, she hurried down to the lobby.

The flowers were sitting on the front counter, a bouquet large enough to all but block out the receptionist seated behind them.

"Um, I heard these might be for me," Talon said as she approached. "Were they just delivered?"

"Not too long ago," Riley, the receptionist, confirmed. "I was about to call you."

"Was it a tall, dark-haired guy with beautiful green eyes who dropped them off?" Talon asked.

Riley laughed. "No, it was a short, wiry woman with mousy brown hair and about a dozen more deliveries before lunch."

Talon nodded. That made sense. She was just kind of hoping maybe Zack had stopped by in person before leaving town. She dug into the arrangement and extracted the miniature card held by the upright plastic fork.

Talon,

Thanks for a wonderful time in Tacoma. I hope you enjoy the flowers. Maybe I'll be back in town before you need a new bouquet.

XO, Zack

"XO?" Talon questioned aloud.

"It means hugs and kisses," Riley offered. "That's nice."

"I know what it means," Talon snipped back. She was just surprised by it. It seemed a little mushy. Or maybe not mushy enough. Probably better than drawing a little heart. Definitely better than the word 'Love.' She frowned. It was probably exactly right. Damn him.

Riley looked like she was about to make another comment when the phone suddenly rang. Riley expertly assessed which number the caller had dialed to reach the shared reception desk for all of the tenants in the office building, then pressed a button, winked at Talon, and answered, "Law Office of Talon Winter. How may I help you?"

Riley kept eye contact with Talon as she nodded along to the speaker. "Yes. Of course. One moment, please. Thank you."

She placed them on hold. "It's about that yacht club case," Riley explained to Talon.

Talon rolled her eyes. "Take a message. I'll call Smerk back later."

Riley shook her head. "It's not Mr. Smerk. It's someone from the Tribe. A Ms. Draper. She wants to talk with you. Now."

Oh, crap. Talon's stomach dropped. "I'll take it in my office."

Riley nodded, then returned to the call. "Ms. Winter will be right with you."

Talon hurried to the elevator. Riley knew exactly how long the elevator ride would take her and her phone started ringing as soon as she stepped into her office.

"This is Talon Winter," she answered.

"Hello, Ms. Winter," came the woman's voice on the other end of the line. "This is Charlotte Draper, general counsel for the

Puyallup Tribe. We met previously at the Smerk and Nordblum offices."

"Ms. Draper," Talon replied as warmly as she could muster. "Yes, of course. Nice to hear from you again."

"I was the one," Draper reminded Talon, "who directed that you be put in charge of our litigation against the Commencement Bay Yacht Club."

Talon didn't need the reminder. "Yes, I recall."

"I'm beginning to wonder if that was a mistake," Draper said. "I would like to meet with you. At my office. This afternoon."

Talon knew what the right answer was. "What time should I be there?"

CHAPTER 14

Charlotte Draper's office was in the Tribal Headquarters Building, a red brick structure located on Portland Avenue, on the other side of the freeway and up the hill from the Port of Tacoma. There was ample parking in the lot out front. Talon found a spot near the door and walked inside exactly five minutes early for her meeting. She didn't mind waiting, and she knew not to make Draper wait.

Draper didn't make Talon wait either. At 12:59, she walked into the lobby and greeted Talon.

"Ms. Winter. Thank you for coming." She shook Talon's hand, then gestured toward the hallway she had emerged from. "My office is right this way."

Talon followed Draper down a hallway of offices, each occupied by another member of the tribal government. Every government agency, state or federal, municipal or tribal, needed the people who sit at their desks and put in the work of deciding how best to steward their community. These were the people doing that for Talon's tribe. And Draper's office was one of the big ones at the end of the hall. The office the people in the other offices went to when they needed help. Or they were in trouble.

"Have a seat, Ms. Winter," Draper directed, gesturing to one of the overstuffed leather guest chairs on the opposite side of her desk.

"Please, call me Talon," Talon insisted as she sat down in the nearest chair.

Draper smiled and nodded. "And you can call me Charlotte."

That was a bit of a relief. Talon wasn't looking forward to some uncomfortable conversation with asymmetrical forms of address. It could just be uncomfortable on the merits.

Draper nodded to herself for a moment, her mouth curling into a half-smile. "This is a big responsibility, isn't it? Representing your own tribe in a landmark effort to reclaim some of our historical land?"

"I like big challenges," Talon answered. "It's why I volunteered for the case."

Draper nodded. "And we're all glad you did. Especially after the other side tried to recruit you."

"Tried to trick me," Talon expounded. "Tokenize me."

"Yes." Draper nodded again. "I imagine that made you angry."

Talon considered. "It made me feel like they underestimated me, and I don't like being underestimated."

"Is that why you volunteered?" Draper asked. "To show them they had underestimated you?"

"It wasn't the only reason," Talon answered, "but it was one of them."

"It's personal," Draper suggested.

"This is my tribe," Talon answered. "That already made it personal."

But Draper tipped her head back and forth equivocally.

"Yeah, but that's not quite the same is it? I mean, it's one thing to want to help your community. It's another to want to show someone up personally."

Talon wasn't sure she agreed, but she could tell she shouldn't argue either.

"I think that can be a great motivator," Draper went on. "That's what I saw at our meeting. That's what I saw when I suggested putting you in charge of the litigation."

"Thank you," Talon said.

"But I think that's also what I saw when I was informed that we are now facing a motion to dismiss our entire lawsuit over an allegation of professional misconduct by you."

There's always a 'but', Talon thought with chagrin.

"Yeah, about that." Talon raised a finger to explain, but Draper cut her off with a sharp wave of her hand.

"If you're going to tell me you didn't do anything wrong, save your words. I'm sure you didn't. That's not the point. The point is that you did something that allowed the other side to accuse you of doing something wrong, and now we have to deal with it."

Talon could hardly argue with that.

"Look, if it's about fees," Talon said, "we won't bill you for dealing with this. It's on me. I'm not in this to make a buck."

"I would only expect as much, Talon," Draper responded. "So that's of little comfort. My concern is that you're treating this like your case when really it's our case." She gestured at her office and the land and people beyond it. "You need to remember that. This isn't some criminal case where you know better than your client and can make all the decisions. We don't need an itchy trigger finger on a half-cocked gun. We need a steady hand on a surgical sword."

Nice metaphors, Talon admired.

"And I need to know which one you are," Draper put to her.

"Sword," Talon replied immediately. Perhaps a little too quickly, she realized. More half-cocked than steady. She took a breath and stared directly into Charlotte Draper's eyes. "A steady hand on a surgical sword. I will win that motion to dismiss and then I will win the case."

Draper frowned slightly. It was obviously what she expected to hear. "I hope so." Then she stood up. "And I hope you know what will happen if you don't. Thanks for coming by."

The meeting was over. Talon was relieved. She had definitely had worse client meetings. She thanked Draper and turned to show herself out. When she reached the door, though, Draper called out, "Was it worth it? Whatever you were trying to accomplish at the yacht club that night? Did you accomplish it?"

Talon smiled back at her. "Of course."

CHAPTER 15

Riley had put the flowers on Talon's desk, off to one side so as not to block her work space, with the vase turned so the greens were nearest the door, leaving the full beauty of the bouquet to be best appreciated when seated in the chair only Talon sat in. Talon took one look at them and dialed Zack's number.

"Talon!" he practically sang her name when he answered the phone. "I was hoping I might hear from you. How's your day going today?"

"Mixed," Talon answered. "At best."

"Oh," Zack's tone dropped a bit. "Well, did something good happen today? It was supposed to have happened by now."

"That's why I'm calling," Talon started to explain.

"Oh, good," Zack's song-like tone returned. "You're welcome."

"You haven't done anything yet." Talon was puzzled by his statement. "We'll see if I thank you."

There was a moment's hesitation on the other end of the line. "Did the flowers not show up?"

"Hm? Oh, yeah, they showed up," Talon confirmed. "They're on my desk. So, listen, I need you to send me that picture you took at the yacht club."

"Um, okay," Zack stammered. "The one of the old guy at the table with that huge lawyer guy?"

"Yeah, that one," Talon answered. "You forgot to send it to me before you left town. Nice of you to mention leaving town, by the way. That was great to learn from Curt."

"I'm pretty sure I mentioned it," Zack defended. "Then again, we didn't do a lot of talking once we got back to your place, if you remember."

Talon sighed. "Can you just send me the photo please?"

"Of course," Zack was quick to agree. "What are you going to do with it? Is there anything I can do to help?"

"No, sorry," Talon answered. "This isn't what Zack Claymore is for. This is a job for Curt Fairchild."

* * *

"Can you identify him?" Talon was standing in Curt's office ten minutes later after finally getting Zack off the phone and waiting far too long for him to get around to sending her the photo of Grainsley's mystery companion.

"From a single low-res camera pic?" Curt asked her.

Talon nodded. "Yes."

Curt smiled broadly. "Of course. No problem. How soon do you need it?"

"Yesterday," Talon quipped. "Or maybe just earlier this afternoon right after lunch. But I need it as soon as possible. Can you do that?"

"I wouldn't expect anything less from you," Curt said. "I was pretty sure what your timeline would be when I asked." He looked at the clock. "It's already after three. I will try to get it done today, but no promises. More likely, it'll be waiting for you on your desk when you get in tomorrow morning." He smiled weakly.

"Right next to the flowers from Zack."

Talon noticed the weakness of the grin. "I'm not really into flowers," she offered.

"I told him that," Curt said. "But you know Zack."

Talon thought for a moment. "Not really. But I guess I'm learning."

"He's a good guy," Curt assured, "and flowers are usually a pretty safe go-to."

Talon frowned. "I'm not looking for safe."

"What are you looking for?" Curt asked, his smile flickering just a little stronger.

Talon pointed at his phone, and the image she had sent to it. "The name of that guy. And why he was having dinner with my opponent."

CHAPTER 16

The next morning, Talon arrived at her office fully expecting Curt to have identified the man in the photograph. Name, address, blood type, everything. Curt was a man of his word, and a hell of an investigator, Talon had to admit to herself, even if she might never admit it to him. However, instead of that welcome sight on her desk, she was greeted with the very unwelcome sight of Amelia Jenkins's sister and brother-in-law in her lobby again. Unwelcome, because she knew exactly why they were there.

"I am so sorry," she apologized preemptively. "I told Amelia I would visit her yesterday after court and then I didn't. That is on me, one hundred percent. Mea culpa. I dropped that ball and I am sorry."

Jennifer Bourdain's scowl did not soften. "Did we make a mistake hiring you?" she demanded. Hank was standing behind his wife, arms crossed. He punctuated her question with the raise of a doubting eyebrow.

"No," Talon assured them. "No, you did not."

"Then why are you still here?" Jennifer asked.

That, Talon agreed, was a very good question.

She pointed at Jennifer Bourdain, then her husband, then

nodded and turned on her heel. She could be at the jail in less than ten minutes.

* * *

"I was wondering if I was ever going to see you again," Amelia said as she dropped into the chair on the other side of the plexiglass from Talon. "I know you're the big important lawyer and everything, but it's my ass that's going to prison if we lose."

"Then we won't lose," Talon responded.

But bravado required buy-in from its intended audience in order to work. Talon had damaged their relationship, and Amelia had little choice but to become her own top protector. "Good idea. Tell me how you plan to do that. Because right now, I'm thinking maybe you're all show until the money hits, then you're a no-show."

There were a few ways Talon could respond. She could apologize again. Well, it would be a first apology to Amelia—and she did need to do that—but it would be the second to the family and while apologies could show strength when it took courage to offer one, they could also suggest weakness when delivered in too large of numbers. No one wanted a weak attorney.

Another option was to lean into the attorney role and take charge. Tell Amelia to trust her—insist on it, really. After all, what choice did she have? They had already paid her. Was she really going to go back to Blondie Wheaton and his plea bargain? Remind Amelia who was boss, and put her in her place. It wasn't the first time an attorney had more important things to do than visit some needy client in jail, and it wouldn't be the last. Suck it up and do as you're told.

Or there was the third option. Talon chose the third option.

"Okay," she answered. "Here's how we're going to win. This is going to take a while to explain, so get comfortable."

Amelia's hardened expression held for a moment, then she leaned forward.

"By the way," Talon added, "I'm sorry."

Amelia waved it away. "Whatever. Explain to me how we're going to win."

So Talon did.

CHAPTER 17

"Andrew Bennington," Talon read the name off the top of the several-page dossier Curt had prepared for her when she finally got to her desk later that morning. He had left it perfectly centered on her desk. Zack's flowers were starting to wilt.

"Andrew Bennington the Third," Curt corrected.

"Third of his name," Talon added, "eater of seafood, client of opposing counsel, stealer of native land."

"Executive assistant to the C.E.O. of Commencement Bay Yacht Club Holdings, LLC," Curt offered his actual title. "He's been the executive assistant to every C.E.O. for the last thirty-two years."

"He knows where the bodies are buried," Talon knew.

"If anyone does," Curt agreed. "And if there are any bodies."

Talon nodded darkly. "Oh, there are bodies, Curt. That's kind of the entire point."

Curt shifted his weight uneasily. He was still standing, halfway between the doorway and Talon's desk. He'd waited for her to arrive, then scurried into her office almost immediately afterward. He obviously wanted to see her reaction to his hard work. It was almost cute. But it was mostly annoying. "Yeah, I guess that makes sense. Sorry."

Talon looked up. "For what?"

Curt rubbed the back of his neck. "Um, colonialism?"

Talon shook her head at him. "Yeah, that's one-hundred percent your fault. But now that you've apologized, we should all be able to move on."

Curt didn't say anything. His eyes darted around uncertainly.

"I'm fucking with you, Curt," Talon let him off the hook. She tapped the folder. "Thank you for this. Now I know why Grainsley was meeting with him. And I know why he got so upset that I might have overheard them."

She also knew who she was going to use her one deposition on.

CHAPTER 18

It was starting to feel a bit like whiplash, swinging back and forth between the civil case of a lifetime—generations of lifetimes—and the criminal case about a real person's actual lifetime. Having figured out why Grainsley was so upset and what to do to make him even more upset, Talon turned her attention back to the matter of *The State of Washington versus Amelia Jenkins*. She had told Amelia what the plan was. It was time to start executing.

Step one was a meeting with the prosecutor. Ostensibly to discuss possible resolutions, but Quinlan wasn't going to offer any better than the plea bargain Wheaton had prematurely agreed to. Quinlan wouldn't want to reward Talon for interjecting herself and canceling the guilty plea, especially not the way she did it. But the meeting wasn't about begging for a better offer. It was about starting the setup for the real battle. The one that would play out in front of the jury.

"Is Mr. Quinlan expecting you?" asked the receptionist at the Pierce County Prosecutor's Office. They actually had several different offices located in several different buildings, one for each of their different divisions—juvenile, misdemeanors, even civil litigation for when someone sued the county over a faulty road or whatever—but the main office, the heart of any county district attorney's office, was the criminal felony division, and that was located on the ninth floor of that same County-City Building the other civic leaders occupied. The public defenders were housed in rented office space three blocks down the hill. God forbid the heroic prosecutors—*'Eric Quinlan on behalf of The People'*—might have to travel more than a comfortable elevator ride to courtrooms where they could railroad innocent people to prison for the sake of supporting the Thin Blue Line standing between them and getting a real job.

"Generally or specifically?" Talon asked the receptionist. "Generally, I'm sure he's expecting me. Specifically, no, I do not have an appointment. But I bet he'll make time for me. Tell him it's Talon Winter."

The receptionist nodded. She was a young woman in her early twenties, dressed just formally enough for a job in a prosecutor's office, but with natural hair pulled back in a loose bun. "I know who you are, Ms. Winter."

Well, that was nice, Talon supposed. Probably. Maybe.

"I'll see if he's available," the receptionist continued. "He's usually in his office. I'll just confirm he's not too busy to see you."

Talon thanked the young woman, then set her briefcase on one of the waiting room chairs, smiling slightly at the receptionist's choice of words. The thing about being an officious douchebag was that it wasn't just for court. It was Quinlan's personality. He was likely as popular with his own coworkers, especially the office staff he probably didn't give two thoughts about—see, 'douchebag', *supra*—as he was with the defense bar. The receptionist seemed to confirm that. 'He's *usually* in his office.' 'I'll *confirm* he's not too busy to see you.' Yeah, Quinlan wasn't winning any popularity contests.

After a few minutes, the receptionist returned and seemed very pleased to tell Talon, "Mr. Quinlan will be out to see you in a moment, Ms. Winter."

It took seven minutes, but eventually Eric Quinlan emerged into the lobby from the door that led back to the secure offices of the county's favorite attorneys.

"Talon," he said with as much venom as those two syllables could carry.

"Eric." Talon returned the venom.

"The Jenkins case?" Quinlan inquired.

"Yep," Talon confirmed.

Quinlan sighed, but then he pushed open the door. "Fine, but let's make this quick. I have a lot to do today."

Talon threw a glance at the receptionist who responded with a knowing smile. *Yeah, Mr. Popularity.* Hopefully the jury would get enough time with Quinlan to feel the same way about him as his coworkers did.

Quinlan took Talon down the maze of corridors that led to his office. Despite its prime location in the courthouse, the interior of the office space was typically government-issue dreary. True public servants didn't spend time or money on decorations. That would require personality, something not always in abundance with people who chose a career of enforcing rules on others. As a result, the hallway walls were off-white and bare, and the carpet had that institutional speckled gray design designed to hide how dirty it might be. Things got a little better when they arrived at Quinlan's office. At least he had decorated it. But he was a douchebag, so that was the central unifying motif of the décor.

Quinlan sat at his desk and Talon sat opposite him, although he didn't bother to invite her to sit. His desk was completely clear, not a single file or even a piece of paper. Clearly a very busy man.

"Let's get right to it," Quinlan began. "I can offer you the same reduction in charges I gave Wheaton, but I'm going to need an extra month in prison. I can't reward her for striking the plea."

"Of course not," Talon replied. "How dare a defendant not recognize your generosity in reducing the charges from a crime she didn't commit to another crime she also didn't commit, but with a lower penalty? The ingratitude is, quick frankly, appalling."

Quinlan's face held its normal humorless expression. "Funny. No, that's really funny. I'm sure the jury will love it when they convict your client as charged and send her to prison for a decade."

So much for the small talk. "Your cops are lying," Talon said. "They were harassing a homeless guy and when Amelia stopped to film them, they lost their shit. She wasn't trying to assault anyone. She was just trying to get away."

"Well, that's a crime too," Quinlan argued.

"What? Failure to obey an officer?" Talon laughed. "That's a misdemeanor. She's already served more than the maximum penalty for that. Cool. You amend to that, she'll plead to it this afternoon and be home in time for dinner."

"I'm not amending to a misdemeanor, Talon," Quinlan groaned. "She nearly killed a police officer."

"A police officer who jumped in front of her moving car," Talon countered. "He should have been killed, and it would have been his fault. The only reason he's not dead is because my client slammed on the brakes so she wouldn't hit him. That's the opposite of intent to assault."

Quinlan shrugged. "That's not how the officers described the incident."

"Allow me to repeat," Talon said. "Your cops are lying."

Quinlan pulled himself up formally. "I don't appreciate that sort of insinuation, counsel."

Talon thought for a moment, just to confirm she'd said what she thought she'd said. "It's not an insinuation, Eric. I'm telling you outright, very specifically. Your. Cops. Are. Lying."

"Good luck proving that in court," Quinlan scoffed. "The word of three cops against the word of an attempted cop-killer? I like my odds."

Talon smiled, coldly. "Interesting you should say that. See, I was thinking. If a cop is willing to lie to cover up their own misconduct—harassing the homeless guy, I mean. Are you following me?"

She didn't want to lose him. The best and brightest in law school didn't usually pursue the prosecutor career path. It was definitely more of a B- student track.

"I follow you," Quinlan answered. "I disagree, but I follow."

"Okay, good." Talon continued. "If a cop is willing to lie to cover up their own misconduct, then I bet they've committed misconduct before, and I bet they've lied about it before. Now here's the big part," she raised a finger to punctuate her point, "and they probably got away with it, which means they would be willing to lie again."

Quinlan just blinked at her. "You're just guessing. There's no way any judge would allow that sort of wild speculation at trial."

"Oh no, of course not," Talon agreed. She reached into her briefcase and extracted the prosecutor's copy of the pleadings she would be filing on her way out of the courthouse after her meeting. "That's why I'll be serving a subpoena on the police department for the personnel files of each of your cops, including any internal affairs investigations. I'm guessing at least one of them has been caught lying before. Then it's not speculation. It's a pattern."

"It's a fishing expedition!" Quinlan snatched the document

out of Talon's hand and stared at it wide-eyed. "The officers have a privacy right in their personnel files. We don't just hand them over because you have a hunch."

"In my opinion, you should be handing them over as a matter of course in every criminal case," Talon responded. "The fact that you don't just suggests that you know there's something there worth hiding. I intend to confirm that, then tell the jury."

Quinlan dropped the papers on his desk and crossed his arms. "If you do this, no deals. I'll pull the offer and your client can lose at trial."

Talon smiled and shook her head. "Oh, Eric, weren't you listening? I already rejected your offer. I already know I'm going to try this case. And I know I'm going to win."

CHAPTER 19

Talon filed her motion to produce the officers' personnel records at the clerk's office on her way out of the building. She knew the police department would ignore a simple subpoena signed by her, even though the court rules gave attorneys the power to demand records themselves. The cops wouldn't ignore a signed order from a judge, though. Well, they would try, but it would be a lot harder. But first she'd have to convince the judge to sign it at the hearing on her motion to compel.

But before that hearing, she had a different hearing, where she would have to convince a different judge not to sign the proposed order of dismissal proffered by Peter Grainsley. Talon wasn't particularly looking forward to seeing Grainsley again, except that she could also issue subpoenas in a civil case, and specifically a subpoena to appear for a deposition. That document was drafted and ready to go, hidden away in her briefcase, when she arrived before Judge Masters for oral argument on 'Defendant Commencement Bay Yacht Club's Motion to Dismiss for Egregious Professional Misconduct'.

'Egregious'. Talon had had to fight the urge to include a rolling eyes emoji in her response brief. But she managed to keep

her argument to the law and, more importantly, the facts. First, she didn't hear a damn word. And second, how could the Court find that she had eavesdropped on an attorney-client conversation when Grainsley had failed to identify how the man he was having dinner with was actually connected with his client, the yacht club? Talon knew he was, thanks to Curt, but it wasn't her burden of proof. The judge, Talon had argued in her brief, should hardly just take the word of a lawyer for one of the parties to the proceedings. Especially that party. Especially that lawyer.

Speak of the devil, or the devil's advocate anyway, Grainsley lumbered into the courtroom two minutes before Masters was scheduled to take the bench. Talon had been there three minutes already. Neither of them wanted to engage in small talk with the other. When Grainsley reached his counsel table at the front of the courtroom, he grunted slightly in her general direction. She replied with a barely perceptible nod.

Neither of them had a client representative with them. Grainsley was hardly going to show up with the man whose identity he was hiding, and Talon hardly wanted Charlotte Draper, or anyone else from the Tribe, staring holes in the back of her head while she staved off the potential death of everything they had been fighting for over the last two years, before she inserted herself into the cause. She still believed she was right to do what she'd done, or at least not wrong. But she knew everyone else was starting to doubt her.

Except Grainsley. Grainsley was scared shitless. Talon decided to focus on that.

"All rise!" the bailiff called out. "The Pierce County Superior Court is now in session, The Honorable Winnifred Masters presiding."

"Please be seated," the judge instructed as she took the

bench. She smiled down at the litigants. "I didn't expect to see you two again until the trial date. Wishful thinking, huh? Well, I suppose I should have known better. This probably won't be the last time either, I would wager."

"It could be, Your Honor," Grainsley interjected, "if the Court grants our motion to dismiss."

Judge Masters sat up a bit straighter and lost the grin that had creeped onto her lips. "Of course, counsel. I did not mean to suggest I had prejudged your motion. I was only attempting to comment on the unplanned nature of the hearing. A rather clumsy attempt, I see now." She cleared her throat. "Perhaps it's best if we get right to it, then, hm?"

Both lawyers quickly agreed, being sure to perform the formality of standing to address the judge. Masters nodded down to Grainsley. "This is your motion, Mr. Grainsley. I will hear first from you."

Talon sat down again while Grainsley remained standing to deliver his argument from behind his counsel table.

"Thank you, Your Honor," he began. "This is a motion to dismiss the cause of action brought by the Puyallup Tribe of Indians against the Commencement Bay Yacht Club for egregious and irreparable misconduct by lead counsel for the Tribe. We understand that dismissal is an extraordinary remedy, to be reserved for the most extraordinary misconduct, but the actions of Ms. Winter rise to that very high level, and indeed surpass it significantly."

Talon considered that eye roll emoji again, but knew better than to actually roll her eyes in open court. Judge Masters wouldn't like it. It would be unprofessional, and that was what she was being accused of. No need to spot Grainsley any points.

"There is no more carefully guarded, no more sacred

privilege than the attorney-client privilege, Your Honor," Grainsley continued. "The caselaw is replete with exceptions to every other legally recognized privilege. The doctor-patient privilege, the priest-penitent privilege, the marital privilege—each of these has been limited in one way or another when the interests of justice have butted up against the policy purposes behind keeping such communications privileged. But not the attorney-client privilege. In every instance, in every challenge, when the interests of justice might otherwise suggest bending the rule, carving out a limited exception, or otherwise weakening the privilege, the privilege has won out. It is probably not an accident that the judges who have safeguarded the absolute sanctity of the attorney-client privilege were themselves lawyers, but I would submit this is not some sort of professional favoritism, but rather stems from a deep and passionate understanding of the foundational importance of a client being able to have an absolutely unconditionally confidential communication with their attorney."

Talon looked around to see if a flag was waving somewhere behind Grainsley. Apparently not, but he was definitely full of a lot of hot air. Still, it was good to scout out her opponent prior to the trial. Assuming, of course, she got to the trial. Grainsley continued his effort to prevent that eventuality.

"The exceptions carved out of the other privileges," Grainsley expounded, "came about in instances when the privilege had been violated but the Court could not bring itself to dismiss the case because of the other equities of the cause. Not so with our cherished attorney-client privilege. In every case where the privilege has been violated, the courts have seen fit to dismiss the cause of action entirely. This only makes sense. If I eavesdrop on a communication between a doctor and his patient or a priest and his parishioner, then I have gained evidence, but nothing more.

However, should I dare to eavesdrop on a privileged communication between my opposing counsel and my opposing party, well, then I have upended our entire system of justice. I have gained access to the innermost thoughts and plans of the other side. This is always unfair. This is always prejudicial. This always results in dismissal."

Talon frowned. He wasn't wrong.

"In this case, Your Honor." Grainsley continued, "and I can scarcely believe I have to make this accusation in open court, but here we are. In this case, Your Honor, Ms. Winter not only intercepted privileged attorney-client information, but she did so by coming to the property of my client, surreptitiously, and lying in wait to unleash her nefarious plan.

'Nefarious'. Talon supposed if she had a mustache she should twirl it. It was getting harder and harder not to roll her eyes.

"It might be one thing, Your Honor," Grainsley said, "if such a conversation was happened onto by chance, or even opportunity. Perhaps something said in the washroom when they thought no one else was present, or written communications left out in the open during a break in trial proceedings. Ms. Winter is undoubtedly aware of that case."

Talon had to nod slightly. She was aware of it. *State v. Granacki*, 90 Wn.App. 598 (1998). She'd cited it more than once in her own efforts to get criminal cases dismissed. It never worked for her. She hoped it wouldn't work for Grainsley either. But it was a good case for him.

"In *Granacki*, a first degree robbery case was dismissed," Grainsley explained, "because a detective, not even one of the lawyers, read the defense attorney's notepad during a recess. The case was *dismissed*. A serious felony criminal case was dismissed because a detective, not even the prosecutor, glanced at a few notes on a legal pad. If the courts can dismiss such a serious case because of a second-hand violation of the attorney-client privilege, certainly a civil suit can be dismissed when the opposing lawyer sneaks surreptitiously into the very business she is suing in order to intentionally and flagrantly violate the privilege."

Talon shook her head slightly. She couldn't have been both surreptitious and flagrant.

"For these reasons, and more as presented in our written briefing, the Commencement Bay Yacht Club respectfully, but confidently, requests this Court to dismiss the case brought against it by Ms. Winter's client, the Puyallup Tribe of Indians. Thank you."

Talon nodded a few more times to herself and rose to her feet even as Judge Masters turned to her and asked, "Response, Ms. Winter?"

"Thank you, Your Honor," Talon said. "As I listened to Mr. Grainsley's advocacy, I was reminded of that old gem of lawyerly advice. 'If the facts are against you, pound on the law. If the law is against you, pound on the facts. And if the facts and the law are against you, pound on the table.' Mr. Grainsley spent essentially his entire argument arguing the law, except at the very end when he made a conclusory factual assertion that I had done the act that the law would require for any of it to actually matter. He pounded on the law. But that's because the facts are against him."

She glanced over at Grainsley, but he was staring at his legal pad, ignoring her. That was fine with Talon. She had ways of keeping him engaged even if he wanted to pretend he wasn't.

"I admit that I did go to the restaurant at the Commencement Bay Yacht Club, Your Honor," Talon continued. "I went there on a date, in fact. And yes, I chose that location because I wanted to see what the yacht club looked like. That's just good lawyering. Always visit the scene of the crime, or in this case, the tort. There is no reason I can't go there, any more than Mr. Grainsley should be prohibited from setting foot on Puyallup tribal land. So, yes, I was there, but that's as far as Mr. Grainsley's facts go, and that is not nearly far enough for any relief, let alone the admittedly extraordinary relief of a dismissal."

She gestured toward Grainsley. "Mr. Grainsley has asserted that he was meeting with a representative of his client, but at no time has he identified this person or how they qualify as a representative of the yacht club. It's not in Mr. Grainsley's brief and he failed again here today to name this person who is allegedly a principal of his corporate client. Who is he, Mr. Grainsley?" Talon asked him directly. "Please, tell us who this oh-so-important representative of your client is."

Grainsley looked up, but not at Talon. "Your Honor?" he said to the judge.

"Ms. Winter," Judge Masters admonished, "you will address your comments to the bench and not to opposing counsel."

That was the rule. It prevented court hearings from devolving into shouting matches between attorneys. Talon knew the rule. She was just trying to make a point. She had succeeded. She moved on.

"More importantly, Your Honor, Mr. Grainsley's assertion that I overheard any conversation between him and his mystery dinner companion is belied by the fact that we were four tables apart from each other and I left as soon as I saw him. Not because I knew he was meeting with a client. I just didn't want to be in the same room as him. Not while I was on a date."

Another gesture toward Grainsley. "Go ahead. I would invite the Court to inquire of Mr. Grainsley. He will admit that we were too far apart for either of us to hear the other, and he will admit I left almost immediately after he was seated. He will answer those questions, even if he won't tell us who his alleged client was."

It was time to wrap it up. Masters didn't seem to appreciate being told to interrogate Grainsley. Judges rarely enjoyed being told what to do. They told other people what to do. That's why most of them wanted to become judges in the first place.

"So, yes, Your Honor, I'm pounding on the facts," Talon summarized. "That's because the law doesn't matter if the facts necessary for it to be triggered simply do not exist. I went on a date. I wanted to see what the club looked like. I saw Mr. Grainsley and his mystery companion. I didn't hear anything they said and I left. Those are the facts. All the law in the world won't change those facts. And therefore, Your Honor, the Court must deny the defendant's motion. Thank you."

Masters thanked Talon back and looked again to Grainsley. "Any reply, Mr. Grainsley?"

Grainsley stood up and pursed his lips for several seconds. Finally, he answered, "No, Your Honor. I think the written and oral arguments I have already made explain why the Court should dismiss the case. I'd rather not get into a tennis match with Ms. Winter, where she tries to depose me through the Court asking questions for her. I don't think any of us want that. My client just wants justice, Your Honor, and in light of everything that has transpired, justice demands dismissal. Thank you."

Coward, Talon thought. He didn't want to have to answer who the man at dinner was.

Grainsley sat down again and it was time for Judge Masters to speak.

"First of all, I'd like to thank both lawyers for their advocacy. I know cases like this one, with so much at stake for both parties, can lead to stressful situations and heated arguments. You were able, for the most part, to focus on the issue at hand."

Talon knew the '*for the most part*' was directed at her.

"It is rare," Judge Masters continued, "that I am able to agree with both lawyers, especially when the remedy sought is so completely dispositive of the case, but I find myself in that position, and happily so. Again, I believe it is a testament to the talents of both counsel, so again, I commend your advocacy."

Talon wondered where the judge was going with all this. She wasn't sure how Masters could agree with both of them, but she supposed it was better than only agreeing with Grainsley.

"Mr. Grainsley is correct," Judge Masters said. "The attorney-client privilege is the most protected privilege that exists in the law. I recall one of my law school professors saying the other privileges were suggestions but the attorney-client privilege was scripture. I also agree with Mr. Grainsley's suspicion that it has been upheld so strenuously because the ones deciding whether to uphold it are all attorneys who understand the absolute necessity of being able to have an honest and frank discussion with a client without fear of the conversation being discovered.

"The remedy for a violation of the attorney-client privilege is not always dismissal," Masters continued, "but there are rarely any remedies short of that which can truly address the wrong committed. The *Granacki* case is instructive. Although it was a criminal case, and therefore other concerns were raised, such as a criminal defendant's constitutional right to adequate and prepared counsel, it is nevertheless instructive that our State Supreme Court felt it necessary that a robber go free rather than countenance a violation of the attorney-client privilege."

Alleged robber, Talon thought to herself.

"So, in this way, Mr. Grainsley is correct," the judge said, "but Ms. Winter makes valid points as well."

Damn right I do.

"As she said, the law favors the yacht club and their motion to dismiss, but the facts seem to weigh in favor of the Tribe. Or rather, the lack of facts."

Talon smiled. *Exactly.*

"To be honest, I find it problematic for an attorney to act as a witness in their own case," the judge continued, "and even more so when the attorney is a witness to their own misconduct, or at least allegations thereof. It raises questions not only of credibility, but professionalism, and the ability of the Court to distinguish between testimony and advocacy."

Talon frowned. *Call me a liar without calling me a liar.*

"But I think I can avoid the problem of relying on factual assertions of one of the attorneys," Judge Masters said. "In fact, I don't believe I need to decide what portions of Ms. Winter's argument were fact and which were law, so to speak, because this motion was brought by the yacht club. The burden of proof is theirs. I would only need consider Ms. Winter's factual assertions if the facts alleged by Mr. Grainsley would, if true, support the finding of a violation of the attorney-client privilege and the remedy of a dismissal."

Or call Grainsley a liar. That's fine too.

"Here, while Mr. Grainsley's recitation of the law is accurate and complete, the facts asserted are conclusory at best, and entirely absent at worst," Judge Masters said. "Mr. Grainsley has failed to identify whom he was having to dinner with or how they are associated with his client. Simply averring the person was a representative of the yacht club is insufficient, I think, because it deprives Ms. Winter of the opportunity to challenge the importance of that person to the organization, and by extension whether the attorney-client privilege would even apply. More importantly, there are no specific facts presented as to how exactly Ms. Winter was able to, or even did in fact, overhear any part of the conversation. I hardly expect Mr. Grainsley to recount a privileged conversation, but there needs to be more, I think, than the fact that everyone was in the same room, especially if that room was a crowded and presumably loud restaurant."

Talon relaxed for the first time since walking into the courtroom. She often wished judges would just start their rulings with a clear 'Granted' or 'Denied' followed by the explanation. But most judges liked to lay out their analysis before finally getting to the conclusion. Doing criminal defense meant usually being on the losing end of that eventual ruling more often than not, but she was enjoying the sensation of seeing a victory slowly approaching as the judge spoke.

"So, in summary," Judge Masters finally got to her ruling, "I find that there are insufficient facts for me to find that the attorney-client privilege was actually violated here. Accordingly, I am going to deny the defendant's motion to dismiss."

Yay.

"However, I do so without prejudice to the defendant to refile the motion with additional factual allegations which would, if true, be sufficient to support a finding that the privilege was in fact violated."

Boo.

"This is a serious allegation," Masters concluded. "I will leave it to Mr. Grainsley to determine whether he believes he would be able to prevail in the future with additional information. "

Double boo. Talon stole a glance at Grainsley to see whether he was smiling at the prospect, but his face was long and serious. She suspected he wouldn't refile the motion because, after all, she didn't actually hear any of their conversation, and he knew it.

"If there is nothing else," Judge Masters invited, "the Court will be at recess."

There was nothing else, and court went into recess. The bailiff and court reporter disappeared to their offices as well, and Talon was left alone in the courtroom with Grainsley. She considered extending a victorious hand and offering a condescending 'Good game', but Grainsley wasn't one to be shaken by that sort of simple mental gamesmanship. Instead, she reached into her briefcase and extracted the 'Notice of Deposition of Andrew Bennington III.'

"Here." She handed it to him. "The deposition is scheduled for a week from today, nine a.m., my office. I'll make the arrangements for the court reporter."

Grainsley looked at the notice for several seconds. "So, you knew the whole time?"

"I figured it out," Talon clarified. "He must be important if you were trying to hide him from me. I'm looking forward to finding out why."

CHAPTER 20

Civil attorneys were so afraid of the unpredictability of trial that they actually conducted their examination of witnesses in advance, with no jury or judge present, in their own offices. That's what a deposition was. Talon recalled doing countless depositions when she was still doing civil practice, and having moved to criminal practice she realized how stupid they were. What good was catching a witness in a lie, or extracting from them a damning admission, if there was no jury there to watch it unfold in real time? All a deposition really did was prepare the witness for those dramatic in-court moments, thereby ensuring they never happened. That was the point. Civil litigation was about settling before trial. But Talon was a trial attorney. Her deposition of Andrew Bennington III would be conducted, not to leverage a settlement, but as preparation for trial.

Bennington arrived ten minutes early. Earlier even than Grainsley, who appeared about five minutes later. Talon appreciated Bennington's punctuality, and Grainsley's unspoken agreement with her to spend as little time together as possible. Riley escorted the two of them into the conference room, where Talon was waiting along with the court reporter who would swear in

Bennington to tell the truth, the whole truth, and nothing but the truth, then take down every word of that alleged truth for later reference.

Talon extended a hand in greeting, but only to Bennington. "Good morning, Mr. Bennington. Thank you for coming here today."

Bennington frowned slightly. "It's not like I really had a choice. You served me with a subpoena."

"I did do that, didn't I?" Talon smiled. "Well, I was just trying to be polite. But we can go ahead and dispense with that, if you'd like. We all have better things to do today, I'm sure."

Talon certainly did. Preparing for the hearing on her motion for those police personnel files came immediately to mind. But everything had its time and place. If she couldn't keep just two plates spinning at the same time, was she even a lawyer?

Bennington frowned at Talon's suggestion. Grainsley grunted. They took their seats on one side of the table, and Talon took hers opposite them. The court reporter was sitting between them, at the end of the conference table. She was a middle-aged woman with tasteful make-up and loose black curls. She had Bennington raise his right hand and asked him if he'd do that 'whole truth' thing.

"I do," Bennington affirmed, then he turned to face Talon. They were ready to begin.

"Please state your full name for the record," she began.

"Andrew Carmichael Bennington, the Third," he answered.

Wow. That was quite the pretentious name, Talon thought. The jury would probably hate him just for his name. Or so she could hope anyway.

"How are you affiliated with the Commencement Bay Yacht Club?" Talon continued.

"I am the executive assistant to the C.E.O., Margaret Robinson," Bennington answered. "Frankly, I'm surprised you're talking to me instead of her."

"I'm sure I'll get a chance to talk to her at some point too," Talon replied.

"You only get one deposition," Grainsley barked. "That was the judge's order. Unless you want to continue the trial and actually conduct discovery properly. I would be agreeable to that."

"I'm sure you would," Talon answered, "but no, this one deposition will be enough. We can talk to everyone else at trial."

Grainsley sighed and grumbled something under his breath. Bennington watched the exchange with a flicker of hope that he might get out of his questioning. But the flicker died and he turned back to Talon for the next question.

"How long have you been the executive assistant to Ms. Robinson?"

Bennington thought for a moment. "Ms. Robinson became C.E.O. almost six years ago."

"And before that, what was your job title?"

"Well, my job title has always been executive assistant to the C.E.O.," Bennington explained. "It's the C.E.O.s who change."

"How many C.E.O.s have you worked for?" Talon inquired.

"Twelve," Bennington knew immediately. "Not all of them lasted as long as Ms. Robinson has."

"How long have you been doing that job?"

"Thirty-two years," Bennington answered. "It was my first job out of college."

Talon nodded. "Wow. How did you get the job in the first place?"

Bennington shifted uneasily in his seat. "My father was the C.E.O."

Talon chuckled. "Of course he was."

That was exactly the sort of real-time exchange that Talon would have wanted a jury to experience firsthand. When they got to trial, Bennington would have figured out a way to package it that didn't reek so obviously of rich kid nepotism.

"What do you do as executive assistant to the C.E.O.?" Talon continued.

Bennington shrugged. "Whatever is needed. A little bit of everything. It's my job to make sure the C.E.O. has the information he or she needs to steward the yacht club successfully until the next C.E.O. takes over."

"Are you good at it?"

Bennington sat up a bit and sniffed. "I like to think so."

"So, for thirty-two years, it's been your job to know everything about the yacht club so the C.E.O. could know whatever it is they might need to know in any given situation," Talon said. "Is that right?"

"I suppose that's right," Bennington answered, with more than a little bit of pride.

"Business records, personnel records, upcoming events," Talon listed possible areas of expertise. "Regalias, I assume?"

"Oh yes, definitely regalias," Bennington confirmed.

Talon shook her head. She was wasting great testimony on a random court reporter rather than the jury who would actually decide whether the pretentious rich kid club should give the land back to the people who first lived on it.

"What is a regalia exactly?" Talon decided to ask. She wasn't going to preview her trial examination for her opponents. She just wanted Bennington to talk to get a feel for his personality and how he would come across at trial.

But Grainsley rained on her parade. "I'm going to object," he interjected. "Mr. Bennington is an executive assistant, not a sailboat captain. There's no foundation for him to answer the question, and in any event, it's irrelevant to the questions at issue in the litigation."

Talon waited a beat. "Are you done?"

Grainsley frowned. "Yes."

She turned back to Bennington. "Okay, go ahead and answer the question. What's a regalia?"

Bennington hesitated. "But Mr. Grainsley objected."

"Yes, he did," Talon agreed. "And the objection was duly recorded by the court reporter. Now you answer the question anyway."

"Really?" Bennington looked to Grainsley for confirmation.

Grainsley sighed. "Yes. If this deposition were to be offered at an actual trial, then the judge would rule on the objection and redact any answers where the objection would have been sustained. But you do go ahead and answer the question for now,"

Bennington thought for a moment. "That seems silly."

"It is silly," Talon agreed. "Now, tell me about regalias. Are there lots of flags and stuff?"

That was how Talon conducted the rest of the deposition, inquiring about tangential matters of doubtful relevancy, just to keep Bennington talking. And also to annoy Grainsley. Anything to annoy Grainsley. Also, by asking Bennington about things he liked and letting him tell her about them, he was naturally going to start liking her. How to Make Friends and Influence People 101 was to ask people about their interests and let them tell you. By the end of the deposition, Bennington would like her, maybe even trust her at an unconscious level. Then Talon would use that to stab him in the face at trial.

It was noon when Bennington finished telling Talon about

his 'gap year' backpacking through South America with nothing more than a change of clothes and thousands of dollars in traveler's checks from his daddy's bank account.

"And that was how I learned the Spanish word for 'infected'!" Bennington laughed. Talon laughed right along with him. Grainsley wasn't laughing.

"Are we going to break for lunch?" he grumbled. A man that size probably couldn't miss many meals, Talon supposed.

"You know what?" she said. "I think we can go ahead and wrap this up. I believe I have all the information I need." She grinned and aimed a finger gun at Bennington. "Even the Spanish word for 'infected'."

More laughter from everyone but Grainsley. Even the court reporter seemed to be enjoying herself.

Talon stood up and extended a hand to Bennington again. "It was a pleasure to meet you, Andrew."

Bennington shook her hand enthusiastically. "The pleasure was all mine, Talon."

Talon smiled. That was absolutely true.

CHAPTER 21

In addition to not wanting to spend any more time with Grainsley, Talon had another reason to end the deposition at noon. Those police personnel files weren't going to turn themselves over. Quinlan wasn't going to turn them over either. And the cops definitely weren't. The hearing on her motion to compel discovery had been special-set for the following Friday in front of Judge Kalamaka. He had started to take a personal interest in the case. Assigning the case to himself would also be a way for him to take a break from the monotony of his current rotation.

So, Talon decided to do a little research on the judge. Would he be pro-cop, pro-defense, or something more tricky like pro-privacy? She needed to know the best way to approach him. Then she'd work that approach into the supplemental brief she was going to drop on Quinlan at the end of the day Thursday.

She found some good background on the Honorable Rodney Kalamaka. He posted a lot on Facebook, probably too much for a judge who was supposed to maintain an appearance of impartiality. He liked every dog photo posted by every attorney he was friends with, which was a lot. Talon didn't think Kalamaka would hold it against her that she didn't have a dog. But she was going to find out if Quinlan had one.

She moved on to general news stories the judge had appeared in, mostly before he became a judge. He hadn't really handled any high-profile cases that had made the local newspaper, but he had done some work for a few different non-profits. There wasn't anything particularly compelling, but she could probably score a point or two with him just by mentioning she had seen his name in the paper. Her perusal of a ten-year-old article about attorney Kalamaka's role in some ill-fated wayward youth center was interrupted by the appearance of Riley in her doorway.

"Ms. Winter? Sorry to interrupt. But I thought you might want to see this right away."

Talon sighed. It was never good when someone thought she should see something right away. "What is it?"

Rather than try to explain, Riley took a nervous step into Talon's office and set the document on her desk. "That very large man just came back and dropped it off. It looked time-sensitive."

"Notice of Deposition of Charlotte Draper," Talon read the caption aloud. "Really? They're going to depose the general counsel? Good luck with that. She knows her way around a deposition probably better than Grainsley."

And better than herself, Talon realized with a frown.

That was going to be awkward. Draper would be able to judge Talon's skills up close and personal. In fact, as Talon considered further, she started to suspect that was Grainsley's reason for choosing Draper—to make Talon look bad in front of her client. When Talon looked at the time the deposition was scheduled, her suspicion was confirmed. Grainsley set it for the exact date and time as her motion to produce the police personnel files.

"God damn it," Talon slammed the paper on her desk and looked up for some encouragement from Riley. But Riley was long gone, having scurried out as Talon examined the deposition notice.

Talon found herself alone. As usual.

Alone, but pulled in every direction by other people. Such was the life of a hard-nosed attorney.

Talon knew there was no chance Quinlan would agree to reschedule the hearing on her motion to compel the police personnel files. He would agree to strike the hearing, and her motion, and never give the records up. But Talon could hardly agree to that.

Similarly, Grainsley would never agree to reschedule the deposition of Charlotte Draper. In fact, he had deliberately scheduled the deposition to conflict with Talon's criminal hearing. Obviously, he had looked up the criminal case online, confirmed the next court date, and then scheduled the deposition opposite it.

Also, it was too late to ask either judge to move the hearing or deposition. To do that, she would have to schedule a hearing on a motion to reschedule—the most lawyer thing ever—and then give the opposing party sufficient notice under the court rules, but by the time she was given notice of the conflict, the deadline for such a motion was already past. Grainsley had timed it perfectly.

That left two possible courses of action. Ask for help, or do it all herself just to spite everyone.

Talon Winter didn't ask for help.

CHAPTER 22

Actually, there was one person Talon could ask for help. The way you ask a dog to get the newspaper.

"Stall them?" Curt shook his head in disbelief. "You want me to stall a room full of attorneys while you're at the courthouse arguing some other motion?"

"Yes. That. Exactly," Talon answered. "I'm glad you understand the assignment."

They were sitting in her car outside Grainsley's office building.

"I understand it," Curt confirmed, "I just don't know how I'm supposed to do it. I think they're going to notice that you're not there."

"Help them not notice," Talon suggested. "Distract them."

"With what? Card tricks?"

"Do you know any card tricks?" Talon asked.

Curt shrugged. "No."

"Okay, then, not card tricks," Talon counseled. "Strike up a conversation with one of them and then just keep it going. Keep talking. Pretend you're that guy at the party no one wants to get cornered by."

Curt thought for a moment. "Dave?"

Talon took a beat. "Sure. Dave. Be Dave, if that's what works for you."

"Dave is the worst." Curt shook his head.

"Perfect," Talon answered. "Be the worst. Be the best. I don't really care. I just need you to go in there and stall them for like an hour. Tell them the ice machine broke. Whatever it takes."

"Why would the ice machine--?"

Talon put a finger on his lips. "You can do this, Curt. I have faith in you."

"You do?"

"Yes."

Curt smiled. "Well, that's nice."

Talon had to smile too. "Yes, actually, it is."

She reached across the car and patted him on the arm, surprised as always by the muscles he kept hidden under his shirt. "Thank you, Curt. I'll be back in an hour."

They both knew it would be longer than that.

* * *

"All rise! The Pierce County Superior Court is now in session, the Honorable Rodney Kalamaka presiding!"

Talon stood up at the bailiff's call, as did everyone else in the courtroom. In addition to the bailiff and the court reporter, there was Amelia at the defense table, two jail guards hovering near the exits, Quinlan at the prosecutor table, and a man who was obviously a lawyer seated in the gallery, two rows directly behind Quinlan. He was a White guy in his 50s, with short gray hair, a dark suit and red tie, indistinguishable from half the local bar. Otherwise, the cavernous courtroom was empty. No one wanted to spend a Friday morning watching a defense attorney crash and burn in a quixotic attempt to hold The Man accountable.

"Are the parties ready," Judge Kalamaka asked, "in the matter of *The State of Washington versus Amelia Jenkins*?"

"The defense is ready, Your Honor," Talon spoke up first. It was her motion.

Quinlan sneered at her. As the prosecutor, he felt entitled to speak first. "The State is ready as well, Your Honor."

The judge raised a chin to the man in the gallery. "And I see we have another attorney present. Mr. Chapman, I believe?"

The man behind Quinlan stood up. "Yes, Your Honor. How nice of you to remember my name."

"Are you here for this case, Mr. Chapman?" the judge asked.

"I am, Your Honor," Chapman confirmed. "I am now the legal advisor for the Tacoma Police Department, so I have a particular interest in the Court's ruling."

The judge nodded at the information. "Do you expect to be heard on the motion?" Kalamaka asked. "I don't believe you're a party to it."

"No, Your Honor," Chapman assured. "I have no standing to address the Court at this time. However, if the Court grants the defendant's motion and issues subpoenas for the officers' personnel records, I have already prepared motions to quash those subpoenas," he patted his soft leather briefcase. "I would be filing those motions immediately upon the Court's ruling."

Great, Talon thought. As if things weren't already stacked enough against her, now there was a mouthpiece for the Blue Line Mafia staring down the judge. Nothing like a little intimidation with your oral argument.

"Well, thank you for coming, Mr. Chapman," the judge said. "It's always good to keep in mind all interested parties when making a ruling."

If Talon hadn't already thought she was probably going to

lose, that comment from the judge seemed to telegraph where things were likely to end up.

"Ms. Winter, this is your motion." Judge Kalamaka returned his attention to the actual litigants before him. "I will hear first from you."

Talon stood up and stole a glance at the clock. They had already wasted precious minutes catching up with Mr. Chapman, legal advisor to the Tacoma Police Department. If Talon was going to lose anyway, she supposed she might as well be quick about it, before Curt started telling knock-knock jokes.

"Thank you, Your Honor. I'm certain the Court has already read my brief on the issue, so I will be concise. We are asking the Court to order the production of the personnel files for the three police officers involved in the incident that led to my client's arrest. My client is charged with a very serious crime, assault in the first degree. That crime carries with it the same penalty as attempted murder. She is facing over a decade in prison, if convicted as charged, despite the fact that she is completely innocent. The reason she sits in court here today, in jail garb with shackles on her wrists and guards at the doors, is because of what those three police officers claimed she did that day. But again, Your Honor, she didn't do what they said she did. Therefore—and there is no gentle way to say this—they are lying. They have lied about what my client did. And if they were willing to lie in this case, it seems likely they have lied in other cases. I don't honestly expect the police department to be concerned about that sort of behavior, let alone surprised by it, but it seems like there is at least some chance they would have investigated it before clearing these officers to return to active duty so they could lie about even more suspects."

"I'm sorry, Your Honor," Quinlan interrupted, "but I feel like I need to object. These sort of *ad hominem* attacks have no place in a court of law. This is a forum to seek the truth, not to trash the reputation of hard-working public servants who put their lives on the line every day to keep the rest of us, even ungrateful criminal defense attorneys, safe."

Speaking of ad hominem *attacks*, Talon thought.

"Your concern is noted, Mr. Quinlan," the judge responded to the objection, "but this is argument on a legal motion and there is no jury here who might be tainted by otherwise inadmissible information. I'm going to overrule the objection. Please proceed, Ms. Winter, although I would agree there is no need for personal attacks."

Talon didn't agree. "Your Honor, I'm just trying to head off a potential prosecution argument that the officers would have been terminated if they were ever found to have lied, and therefore their continued employment is evidence that there are no such allegations or investigations in their personnel files. I submit that is likely not true, and the Court should draw no inferences in favor of the integrity of the police officers just because they are still employed."

Another quick glance at the clock. "The only other thing I would say, Your Honor, is that there is no harm in providing me this information. Not really. Not in comparison to the harm that will be inflicted on Ms. Jenkins if she is wrongly convicted based on nothing more than the word of these three officers. Let me look. If there's nothing there, then fine. But if there is, then Ms. Jenkins is entitled to it. Thank you."

Short and sweet. Often that could carry the day. Talon doubted it would on the day the cops sent their own lawyer into the courtroom to mean mug the judge.

Kalamaka seemed a bit surprised by the brevity of Talon's argument, but he turned to Quinlan and invited, "Response?"

Quinlan popped to his feet. "Yes, Your Honor. Definitely. Gladly." He seemed bolstered by the presence of Mr. Chapman. "This is nothing more than a fishing expedition, Your Honor."

Ah, yes, Talon thought, *the time-honored 'fishing exhibition' smear.* As if there were anything wrong with fishing expeditions. How else were you supposed to get fish?

"Ms. Winter is conflating defending her client with believing her client," Quinlan continued. "Every criminal defendant who doesn't plead guilty—and I would remind the Court that this defendant was scheduled to plead guilty before Ms. Winter got involved—every defendant who claims they are innocent, by definition, is disagreeing with the version of events documented by the police. That's how this works. That's why we have juries to decide who's telling the truth. So, it does not follow, as Ms. Winter argues, that her client's disagreement with the police officer she assaulted necessarily means that the officer is a liar. Quite the contrary, Your Honor. On the one hand, we have three sworn police officers who have provided a consistent, reasonable, believable recitation of the facts. On the other hand, we have a person who assaults police officers and is facing more than ten years in prison. I think it's obvious who's lying in that situation, Your Honor, and it's not the police officers."

Quinlan smiled smugly. He was obviously impressed with his own argument.

"We can't go around turning over private personnel files every time a defense attorney takes issue with a police officer's version of events." Quinlan continued. "That happens in every case. It is literally the job of a criminal defense attorney to challenge the police's version of events. That cannot be the trigger to turning over personnel files, or it would be standard procedure in every case and we wouldn't need special motions like the one we're gathered for this morning."

Quinlan took a breath and gazed quickly around the room, ostensibly to gauge how he was doing. Talon ignored him. She didn't look but she could imagine Chapman giving him an encouraging nod, or even a thumbs-up. In any event, he continued.

"There is no reason to suspect there is any information in those personnel files even close to what Ms. Winter hopes, in desperation, might be there. Perhaps, if there were some actual, concrete reason to believe such information was in any of those files, then maybe, just maybe, the Court could consider violating the officers' right to privacy for some greater good of a defendant's right to a fair trial or whatever."

'Or whatever.' Talon was impressed by the sheer dismissiveness of the comment.

"But there is no such concrete reason here," Quinlan asserted. "There is no reason to believe there would be anything like that in their files, and without that sort of concrete reason, the Court should deny the motion to produce the records. Thank you."

Talon stood up even as Quinlan was sitting down. Not because she was angry and needed to respond immediately. Because she needed to get out of there and back to Grainsley's office.

"I can't know if there's anything relevant in the files unless I can look in the files," Talon explained. "This is the typical response of the State whenever the defense seeks access to records like this. 'You can't look at the records because you don't know what's in the records, and you don't know what's in the records because you can't look in the records.' I can't give anything more concrete because the concrete, if it exists, is hidden in the files I'm asking the Court to let me look at. It's as simple as that, Your Honor, and the Court's ruling should be simple too. Please grant my motion for production of the officers' personnel files. Thank you."

Talon had done a decent job keeping her argument concise. Quinlan hadn't blabbed on either. Chapman had kept his mouth shut. The only thing left to worry about was Judge Kalamaka doing that judge thing of taking forever to explain their ruling. If he started talking about the history of the common law as it related to the parchment-based personnel records of the first shire-reeves of Olde England, she might just have to interrupt and ask the judge to just say 'yes' or 'no' to her motion. She was a busy woman. She had places to go, depositions to defend.

"Thank you, Ms. Winter," Judge Kalamaka began, "and thank you, Mr. Quinlan. This is, as you are both well aware, a difficult question for a court to balance. Ms. Jenkins is entitled to a fair trial and an integral part of that is prepared counsel and effective cross-examination of the State's witnesses. However—"

There was no '*however*', in Talon's estimation. Amelia's right to a fair trial more than trumped whatever garbage Kalamaka was about to say.

"—the officers also have a right to the privacy of their personnel records. Police officers do not give up their own rights when they choose to serve, and it will take more than mere suspicion and conjecture before a court can or should infringe on the rights of those police officers."

Talon tapped her foot impatiently. *Just get to it, Rodney. Everyone knows what you're going to say. This is the battle, not the war.*

"I don't believe the showing necessary to order at least partial production of police personnel records is quite as high as Mr. Quinlan might suggest, but it isn't zero either. Ms. Winter's argument boils down to believing her client over the officers and then concluding not only must they be affirmatively lying, rather than simply mistaken, but further that they must have lied in the past and gotten caught. Quite frankly, that is simply too speculative, too attenuated to rise to the level where production of the requested records is required."

Talon stood up and interrupted the judge's soliloquy. This was why she'd noted the hearing. "What would it take, Your Honor? A demonstrated instance of false testimony? Would that be sufficient?"

Judge Kalamaka frowned at Talon. No judge liked being interrupted, especially when the interruption came across as a challenge. But Kalamaka was basically a nice guy, and nice guys let a lot of things go.

"That would likely be sufficient, yes, Ms. Winter," the judge confirmed. "Do you have that here and just failed to mention it until now?"

Talon shook her head. "No, Your Honor. I don't have that."

Not yet.

"In that case, I will deny the defendant's motion to order the production of the personnel files of the three police officers involved in the case," Judge Kalamaka ruled. He nodded again toward the gallery. "It looks like we won't be needing your motions to quash after all, Mr. Chapman. Thank you for coming."

Thank you for intimidating the judge, Talon sneered.

"My pleasure," Chapman replied. He headed toward the exit, followed closely by Quinlan. The judge and his staff retreated as well.

Talon turned to her client as the guards started closing in on the defense table. "This is what we expected," she said to Amelia. "Remember?"

Amelia nodded. "You predicted it. I guess you do know what you're doing."

"I try to," Talon replied. "They're going to take you back to your cell and I have to go now. We're good, right? We lost, but we're still good."

"We're good," Amelia assured her.

Talon patted her cuffed hand. "Good. I'll come by to visit you soon. It's time to get ready for the trial."

Amelia smiled at her lawyer. "I'll look forward to it."

Talon looked at the clock. It had been almost an hour and a half since she dropped off Curt. She hoped he'd learned a card trick or two after all.

CHAPTER 23

Talon broke several traffic laws on her way to Grainsley's office and parked in a very clearly marked no parking zone directly across the street. She pressed the elevator button approximately two dozen times until its doors finally opened and she rushed inside. When she finally got to the twelfth floor, she threw a 'Good morning!' at the startled receptionist, then rushed into the conference room to a mix of surprise and relief. And annoyance. There was a lot of annoyance in that conference room.

Not from Curt, though. He was firmly in the relief camp.

"Oh, thank God," he gasped. He was standing at the head of the table and positioned such that Talon wondered whether he really had begun resorting to card tricks.

"Nice of you to finally arrive," Grainsley muttered without looking directly at her.

Draper didn't say anything. She just shook her head slightly and the mild frown she was wearing when Talon spilled in turned to a hardened scowl.

"I can leave now, right?" Curt asked, already halfway to the exit. Talon nodded and he turned back to the others to offer a, "Nice to meet all of you," before slipping past Talon and out the door.

"Card tricks?" Talon asked.

"Twenty questions," Draper answered. "We didn't finish the last one, but I suspect it was a bicycle."

Talon relaxed a bit and stepped fully into the room. "Well, allow me to apologize for my late arrival." She cast an eye-dagger at Grainsley. "I got double-booked."

"I was surprised you didn't ask me to delay the deposition," Grainsley remarked, "but you just didn't care about inconveniencing everyone else. I knew you were overconfident. I didn't know you were also rude. Well, not this rude anyway."

"I feel strongly that I'm not the one in this situation who was rude," Talon replied. "Now, shall we get started?"

"Can we talk for a moment in the hallway?" Draper asked. "I'd just like to check in with you before we begin. I didn't get the chance to do that earlier because, well, you weren't here."

"Of course," Talon agreed. She didn't seek Grainsley's approval. He could wait a little longer. The whole thing was his fault anyway.

She and Draper walked through the lobby out to the relative privacy of the elevator bank.

"Are you sure you're ready for this?" Draper began. "I know you had a scheduling conflict, and I know it was Grainsley who set that up, but I'm concerned that when you decided whom to prioritize, we finished second. I hope you at least won your motion."

Talon shook her head. "Nope. I lost."

"You're ninety minutes late and you didn't even win?"

"It's okay," Talon assured her. "I expected to lose."

"You knew you were going to lose and you still made us go second?" Draper lamented. "That does not make me feel good about your level of investment in our case."

"That was court," Talon defended, "with a real judge and everything. This is a deposition. We could do this in a bar."

"It's not even eleven yet," Draper pointed out.

"I'm just saying," Talon replied. "My client on that case is sitting in a jail cell and was transported in handcuffs to the courtroom at the exact time the hearing was scheduled. You got to play twenty questions and could have gone out for a latte. I don't think you want to change places with her."

Draper frowned but conceded the point. "Fine. So what's the play here?"

"The play?" Talon questioned.

"The plan," Draper clarified. "What's our plan?"

Talon narrowed her eyes slightly. "Easy. Tell the truth."

"Well, obviously I'm not going to lie," Draper complained. "You are going to defend this, right? You have to object to preserve the record. I may be a lawyer, but in this deposition I'm the witness. I can't object. You have to do it for me."

"I know how it works," Talon assured her. "I will object as necessary. But don't get too worked up. Grainsley didn't pick you to depose because he thinks you actually have any valuable information."

"Wow. Thanks."

"I just mean," Talon explained, "he picked you, and then jammed up my schedule to make me look bad. He wants you to second-guess putting me in charge. He knows if someone else takes over the case, that person will agree to delay the trial yet again, even if only because they'll need time to get caught up."

"So, what should I do?" Draper asked.

Talon smiled. "Don't second-guess me."

She didn't wait for Draper to agree. She just put a guiding hand on Draper's arm. "Come on. Let's do this."

They walked back into the conference room and Grainsley looked up at them from his seat at the table. "Are we finally ready?"

"We are," Talon answered. She took a seat opposite Grainsley and Draper sat next to her.

Grainsley grunted again and nodded at the court reporter. "Swear her in," he directed.

The court reporter complied. He was a young man in his early twenties, with short hair and an old sweater that would have looked more natural on his grandfather. Draper raised her right hand and swore to tell the truth, the whole truth, and nothing but the truth.

But there were limits to everything.

"Please state your name for the record," Grainsley began. He was reading from a list of questions on his legal pad and didn't bother looking up at Draper as he questioned her.

"Charlotte Draper."

"How are you employed?"

"I am general counsel for the Puyallup Tribe of Indians."

"You're a lawyer?"

"Yes."

A grunt, then, "How long have you been practicing?"

"Eighteen years."

"How long have you been general counsel for the Puyallup Tribe?"

"Seven years."

"Where did you work before that?"

Talon had expected something more interesting than this line of questioning. Grainsley could have just asked for her resume. *This deposition could have been an email with an attachment.*

Draper recited every job she'd had since the legal internship after her first year of law school, then Grainsley moved on to his next area of questioning.

"Married?"

Draper raised an eyebrow at him. "Excuse me?"

Grainsley finally lifted his massive head and looked at her. "Are you married?"

"Why is that relevant?" Talon interjected.

Grainsley swung his head at Talon and sighed. "Is that an objection?"

"Sure," Talon answered. "Objection, relevance."

"Noted." Grainsley nodded and returned his gaze to his notepad. "Answer the question."

"Yes, I'm married."

"How long have you been married?"

Draper paused, then decided to answer. "Fourteen years."

"First marriage?"

"Is it my first marriage?" Draper clarified.

"Yes. Is this your first marriage?"

"Yes, it's my first marriage," Draper answered. "And my last, I hope."

Grainsley ignored the editorial add-on. "How many people did you date before your husband?"

"Objection," Talon interjected again.

This time Grainsley didn't lift that thick head of his. "Noted. Answer the question."

"No," Draper said. "I'm not answering that. It's not relevant."

"That's for a judge to decide later," Grainsley told her.

"I'm not answering that question," Draper repeated.

Grainsley hesitated, but moved on to his next question. "Did you ever cohabitate with anyone, including your eventual husband, prior to your marriage?"

"Are you kidding me?" Draper raised her voice.

"Objection," Talon said again. "Move on, Peter. This isn't relevant to anything and you know it."

"We may need to get the judge involved," Grainsley warned.

"Move on," Talon repeated. "Ask about the case."

Grainsley scowled at her for several seconds, then lowered his gaze to his list of questions again. "You're a member of the Tribe, correct?"

"Correct." Draper tried to calm down a bit.

"But you're not a full-blooded Indian, right?" Grainsley asked. "There aren't any full-blooded Indians anymore, are there?"

"And we're done," Draper announced, standing up.

"Is that an objection?" Grainsley looked up to ask.

"It's a termination of the deposition," Talon answered, also standing. "We don't have to put up with your racist, misogynistic bullshit."

Grainsley leaned back. "Hm. That's problematic. I was granted only one deposition prior to the trial and now you've unilaterally terminated it. I don't how I can be prepared in time for trial now."

Talon scoffed. "Is that what this was? A delaying tactic? Are you that afraid of trial? Are you that afraid of me?"

Grainsley stared Talon in the eye for several seconds, then turned to the court reporter and instructed him to stop taking down their conversation.

"I'm not afraid, Ms. Winter, but I'm in no hurry either. If I could," he explained, "I would delay this trial until the sun goes out. It is in my client's interests for this litigation to remain unresolved. As long as the case is unresolved, things stay as they are, and the way things are is that my client owns the land your client is trying to take away."

Talon almost appreciated the honesty, but really it just made her that much more determined to force the case to trial.

"Now, if you'll excuse me," Grainsley pushed himself to his feet, "I have a motion to draft about a new deposition, reopening discovery, and continuing the trial date, probably into late next year. You can see yourselves out."

CHAPTER 24

Not only did Grainsley file his promised motion for a new deposition, discovery, and trial date, but he also filed another motion to dismiss. *The* motion to dismiss in civil practice. The 12(b)(6) motion to dismiss.

Named after Civil Court Rule 12(b)(6), the motion was a request for the Court to throw out the case prior to trial for 'failure to state a claim upon which relief can be granted.' That was lawyer-talk for, even if everything you say is true, you can't sue over that. The rule was designed to weed out truly frivolous lawsuits—like suing a neighbor for not mowing their lawn often enough, or a store for being closed on Mondays when that's when you like to do your shopping. Since those sort of facially ridiculous lawsuits were exceedingly rare, one would expect motions to dismiss under 12(b)(6) would also be rare. On the contrary, however, they were routinely brought by civil defendants, almost as a matter of course. And why not? If you lost the motion, you were no worse off than you were before, and if you won, the case was dismissed.

The 12(b)(6) motion was the one the civil litigators always got excited about. Litigators, like Grainsley. Not trial attorneys, like Talon. Litigators didn't want to go to trial; that was why they filed

12(b)(6) motions. And that was why they got so worked up about them. They revered them as a sort of mini-trial, despite the complete lack of witnesses or jurors. They would even keep track of how many 12(b)(6) motions they had argued. Talon was arguing motions to dismiss every other week. Counting those would be like counting Tuesdays.

All of that meant that when Grainsley served his 12(b)(6) bombshell on the law offices of Smerk+Nordblum, Talon was summoned to those same offices for an emergency strategy session with both Jason Smerk and Charlotte Draper.

"This is big, Talon," Charlotte intoned as they gathered around Smerk's desk. "We knew this would come eventually, but, well, we hoped we might get lucky and avoid it."

"If we lose this," Smerk added, "we lose the case. Everything. It's over."

"Frankly, Talon," Charlotte put in, "we're very concerned with the way the case is proceeding. You prioritized a criminal motion over my deposition. Your misadventure at the yacht club put the litigation in danger of dismissal. And I'm starting to think Grainsley may have a point about slowing things down so we can do them right. I know I wanted you in charge of this litigation, but I'm not so sure you should argue the 12(b)(6) motion. Do you even remember what they are?"

"Of course," Talon answered. "They're *Knapstad* motions for civil cases."

Charlotte's brow furrowed and she looked to Smerk for elucidation, but he just shrugged.

"*Knapstad* was the case," Talon explained, "where the State Supreme Court established an equivalent procedure to dismiss a criminal case. It's the same standard basically."

Draper and Smerk both frowned. They didn't seem

convinced.

"Look, if anything, doing criminal has honed my understanding of the standard here," Talon told them. "A 12(b)(6) motion is a big deal, right? You don't see one filed until things are getting real. But that same standard is applied literally every day at the first hearing of every criminal case. To get bail, the prosecutor has to win the equivalent of a 12(b)(6) motion. The judge assumes the truth of the State's allegations, draws all reasonable inferences in favor of the State, and then decides whether any rational jury could find the defendant guilty. That's what courts do when they decide the 12(b)(6) motion: could any jury possibly find in favor of the plaintiff? In fact, they're even harder in criminal cases because the evidence has to be enough to convince a jury beyond a reasonable doubt. And that's at the beginning of every single criminal case.

"After that," she continued, "a lot of cases have those *Knapstad* motions I mentioned, so that's basically a second bite of the apple. And of course, after the prosecution rests its case, but before you start the defense case-in-chief, you always make a halftime motion to dismiss. Same standard. Assuming everything the State presented and drawing all inferences in favor of the State, could any jury convict? So really, every criminal case that goes to trial has at least three 12(b)(6) motions baked in."

"Is that true?" Draper asked.

"It's true," Talon answered. "And that's why I'm the person you want to argue this motion. Trust me."

Draper looked to Smerk. Smerk looked back at her. It didn't hurt that Smerk, if he was like most civil attorneys, was intimidated by the thought of arguing a Big Bad 12(b)(6) Motion. Finally, he nodded.

"Okay," Draper assented. "If all of that is true, then maybe you are the best person to argue it."

"Great," Talon replied. "When is it set for?"

Maybe she could knock it out before Amelia's case started.

"Two weeks from Monday."

Or maybe not. That would be smack dab in the middle of the State's case-in-chief.

"Is that a problem?" Draper must have noticed her expression twitch.

"No problem at all." Talon assured.

Maybe Curt could do those card tricks for her criminal jury while she was down the hall saving her civil case from being dismissed.

CHAPTER 25

Talon had some time to draft her reply to Grainsley's 12(b)(6) motion. But time had run out on preparing for Amelia Jenkins's trial. The day of the readiness hearing had arrived. Judge Kalamaka took the bench, looked down at her and Quinlan, and asked, "Are the parties ready for trial to begin on Monday?"

"The State is ready," Quinlan answered first. Talon let him.

She looked to her client and they exchanged nods. "The defense is ready," Talon confirmed.

"Are there any significant scheduling conflicts I should know about?"

There was no way Talon was going to mention needing to argue a silly little 12(b)(6) motion in the middle of an actual criminal trial. Not until she really had to. "None from the defense, Your Honor."

"None from the State," Quinlan added.

"Then this matter is confirmed for trial," the judge announced. "I will see everyone back here Monday morning at nine o'clock to address preliminary motions and begin selecting a jury."

Kalamaka took his leave then, his staff following him out of the courtroom. Quinlan departed as well. It was a quick hearing—a formality, really. Just a check-in to make sure nothing had come up that would prevent the trial from proceeding as planned.

"That makes it very real." Amelia felt the significance of the hearing. "I'm scared now."

Talon had a canned response for when clients told her they were scared. 'Good,' she would say. 'That means you're paying attention.' But that wasn't the right thing to say just then. There was no right thing to say just then. An innocent woman was about to be put at the very real risk of going to prison for a decade.

What did you say to that?

"I know."

CHAPTER 26

The guards dragged Amelia away, mostly figuratively, and Talon made her exit from the courthouse. She was considering whether to pick up a coffee on the way back to her office when she heard a voice call out her name from behind her. "Talon! Talon, wait up!"

Not just any voice. A man's voice. Zack's voice.

She turned around and saw Zack jogging toward her, a not at all unappealing sight.

"What are you doing here?" she asked.

"You didn't answer my texts," he said when he reached her, only slightly out of breath.

"You texted me?" She pulled out her phone and checked. "You texted me once."

"And you didn't reply," Zack said.

"It says, 'Nice day for BBQ'," she read aloud, "and has a picture of some sort of meat on a grill."

Zack grinned. "Okay, you got me. That's not why I came up here. Well, it kind of is. I just wanted to see you again."

That was nice, Talon supposed. A little clingy. Definitely inconvenient. But nice.

"I know you're super busy," Zack went on, "and we can't ever go to that yacht club again, but I was asking Curt if he knew any really good restaurants that maybe you've never been to, and—"

"Curt?" Talon interrupted. "You asked Curt for advice on dating me?"

"Well, no, not dating advice," Zack defended. "Restaurant advice. Just maybe a great place in town that you didn't know about. Something to surprise you with."

"I'm not a fan of surprises," Talon replied. She gestured at the two of them. "Like this, actually. Although it's nice to see you again, I guess."

Zack laughed. "It's nice to see you again too, I guess."

Talon took a moment to try to appreciate the man in front of her. But she could only spare a moment.

"So, wanna grab dinner tonight?" Zack asked.

"Oh, no chance," Talon answered. "No, I've got way too much to do. You were perfect for when I was between trials, but now I have two and I'm pretty sure they're going to overlap. I like you and everything, but I don't have time for a boyfriend. I mean, don't get me wrong. You're definitely boyfriend material. I'm just not girlfriend material."

"You could be," Zack encouraged.

"No," Talon replied firmly, "I'm not. Listen to the woman when she's talking. No."

Zack's broad, muscular shoulders dropped.

"Maybe when I'm done with these cases," Talon allowed. "Probably, even. But not right now."

Zack forced a grin. "Priorities," he said.

"Exactly," Talon agreed. She looked again at the handsome, eager man offering himself to her. "Look, I usually like to release some tension the night before trial. If you're still in town then, maybe we can get together."

Zack looked a little crestfallen at the reduction of their relationship to a booty call. But he didn't say no either.

"In the meantime," Talon said, "you should take Curt to that restaurant. He deserves a good date."

CHAPTER 27

That night found Talon working late in her office. There were always a million little things to do to be ready for trial, and even then, new things always popped up. That was part of the reason it was so important to lock down the predictable things, so there would be capacity in her brain to deal with the unexpected things that were inherent in criminal trial work. The fun stuff.

"Surprise!" Curt called out from her doorway. He held up a take-out bag. "I brought you leftovers."

Talon wrinkled her nose. "Gross."

"Well, not leftovers," Curt clarified. "I had them make a to-go order. It's fresh. I didn't put my mouth on it. Neither did Zack."

"Ah." Talon reconsidered. She had forgotten to eat dinner. The aroma of the food sent a sharp pain through her empty stomach.

"Although maybe you'd be okay with Zack's mouth on it," Curt continued. "I don't know."

Talon raised a stern hand. "Don't."

"Don't what?" Curt asked, still standing in her doorframe.

"We're friends, Curt," Talon said, "but you don't get to know about my sex life."

Curt winced just a bit. "Apparently I get to know enough to know you had sex with him."

Talon shook her head. "Again, don't. Just don't."

Curt stood there for an uncomfortable few moments, then stepped into her office and set the bag on her desk. "It's from a new place called Delmonico's up on MLK."

"Italian?" Talon asked, pulling the bag to her. It didn't smell like Italian.

"Asian fusion," Curt answered. "And craft cocktails."

Talon nodded. "That sounds awesome."

"It is," Curt confirmed. "Thanks for telling Zack to take me there."

Talon smiled at that. She liked it when men did what she told them to do. She opened the bag and extracted the box inside. It was a meat and noodle dish that would have smelled amazing even if she hadn't been starving at that moment. "What is this?"

"It's like a Szechuan filet mignon thing, with broccoli and snow peas, over glass noodles," Curt answered.

"That sounds incredible," Talon said. "It smells incredible."

"Well, I knew you'd be working late," Curt said as he sat down across the desk from her. "And I knew you'd be hungry."

"Thanks, Curt." Talon looked again at her perfect meal and tore open the package of chopsticks. "And thanks for knowing."

"Well, we're friends, right?" he said.

Talon smiled crookedly while swallowing her first bite of the heavenly food. "I wouldn't know what you were doing any given night, and I sure wouldn't know if you were hungry."

"Yeah, I know." Curt shrugged. "So, trial on Monday, huh? Do you feel ready?"

Talon appreciated that he knew not to ask *if* she was ready. Of course she was. The real question was whether she *felt* ready.

That was more complicated.

"I'm getting there," Talon answered. "It's hard with that other case tracking along right after it."

"The yacht club case?" Curt confirmed. "Is that coming up for trial too?"

"In two weeks," Talon answered. "With a motion to dismiss between then and now."

Curt thought for a moment. "You won't be done with this trial in two weeks."

"I know," Talon agreed.

"Are you going to delay one of them?" Curt asked. "Or hand one of them off?"

"Nope."

"Why not?"

"Because that's not what I do."

Curt laughed. "I don't know. You kind of handed that deposition off on me."

Talon smiled. "That's different."

"Why?" Curt asked.

"I don't know," Talon answered. "It just is."

"Because you care about both of these cases," Curt suggested, "but you didn't care about being late and inconveniencing other people."

Talon laughed. "Yeah, that's probably part of it."

"Well, which case do you care about more?"

"They're both important," Talon answered.

"That's not what I asked." Curt raised an eyebrow at her.

But Talon shook her head and raised that stern hand at him again. "Nope. We are not doing this either. We are not doing 'overwhelmed working woman gets career and life advice from male love interest'."

Curt smiled. That eyebrow shot up higher. "Love interest?"

Talon sighed. "Whatever. Focus. I don't need your advice. I care about both cases and I'm going to handle both cases."

"It's okay," Curt said. "I already know which case you care about more."

"Oh, really?" Talon said, her mouth full of Szechuan beef and noodles again. "Because I don't. Please enlighten me."

"It's obvious," he asserted. "The criminal one."

Talon paused chewing just long enough to ask, "And why do you say that?"

"Because you took it even though you knew it would screw up the civil case," Curt explained. "Which it did. My performance at the deposition is Exhibit A."

"Don't flatter yourself," Talon joked. "You're like Exhibit J, at best. Maybe more like Q, or W."

"Exactly," Curt returned. "One of many instances of that criminal case taking precedence."

Talon frowned at the analysis but didn't argue against it.

"It's okay," Curt continued. "I'm not judging you. It makes sense. Criminal law is where your passion lies."

Talon grimaced. "I'm not really a passionate person, Curt," she said. "I just turned down a guaranteed lay with a super-hot firefighter to work on my jury selection questions."

Curt winced again. "I thought we weren't going to talk about your sex life."

"My point is," Talon said, "I'm calculating, not passionate."

"That's what you tell yourself," Curt replied, "but passion doesn't always have to be big and splashy and purple."

Talon cocked her head at him. "Purple?"

Curt forged ahead. "It can also be slow and smoldering, keeping you warm all of the time until you don't even notice it anymore."

"How can it be passion if you don't even notice it?"

"Think about the most beautiful garden you've ever seen," Curt said. "Think about the gardener who gets up every day and tends to that garden, knowing exactly what to do for each different plant during each different season, year after year. You can't do that without passion, but it's the type of passion that burns a lifetime, not just one night or one case."

Talon took a moment to consider Curt's point.

"That's why you took that case," he went on. "Passion."

"I have a passion for winning," Talon said.

"No." Curt shook his head. "You have a passion for justice. And that's the same reason you volunteered for that civil case too. Justice. Passion."

Talon frowned at herself. Maybe they were doing that life advice thing after all. She decided to turn the tables.

"Alright then, Mr. Fairchild," she said. "And what do you have a passion for?"

"Me? Oh, that's easy." Curt smiled. "You."

CHAPTER 28

Sunday afternoon. The day before trial. One last meeting with her client before the tempest began.

Talon did her best to appear calm and in control. Amelia couldn't hide looking stressed and scared.

"We have a plan, right?" Talon reminded her.

"Right," Amelia agreed.

"We're going to win, right?"

"Right."

"And you trust me, right?"

"Right."

That was all Talon could ask for. There wasn't any more preparation she needed to do with Amelia. She just needed her to trust her. Once the trial started, things would move quickly, and in unexpected directions. Talon wouldn't be able to consult with her client before every decision.

"But I do have one question," Amelia said.

"What is it?"

"Why?" Amelia asked.

Talon narrowed her eyes at her. "Why what?"

"Why are you doing this?" Amelia said. "Why did you

speak up when my old lawyer tried to trick me into taking that deal? Why did you take the case when you probably have a million other cases you need to worry about? Why this case? Why me?"

Those were good questions.

Talon had a good answer.

"I guess," she recounted, "I have a passion for justice."

CHAPTER 29

Talon had a routine she followed the night before trial. Every trial lawyer did. Part superstition, part preparation, it was the final moment to center yourself before battle. Talon's routine didn't involve any further work on the case. All of the work was already done. She wasn't going to gain any advantage by looking over her opening statement one more time, or organizing her exhibits yet again. Her routine was about clearing her mind, and her body.

She cinched her robe and poured herself a shot of whiskey. That smoky Japanese brand from the liquor store on Sixth. She walked over to the sliding glass door to her balcony and looked out at the night sky over Commencement Bay. She could see the lights on Anderson Island, and one small winking light making its way slowly across the water. Probably one of those useless fishing expeditions.

The work needed to be completely finished and set aside so that her brain could step away from the distraction of myopically working on an endless series of individual tasks. She could allow her subconscious to slosh around in the entirety of the case all at once. That was how otherwise unnoticed connections were made. That was how bad ideas turned into good ideas. Not because they had changed, but because everything around them had.

Talon finished her whiskey and set the glass in the sink. She walked down the hallway to her bedroom, let her robe fall to the floor, and climbed into her warm bed. He was asleep already. Men always fell asleep afterward. She put her head on his naked chest, wrapped an arm around his waist, and closed her eyes. And smiled.

CHAPTER 30

The first day of trial was filled with preliminary matters. The entire first week, in fact, if either of the attorneys was obstreperous and obstructionist. Talon could be both, if it helped her client. By the time the judge finalized the scheduling, ruled on the standard preliminary evidence motions, and swore in the twelve people selected from the panel of 50 potential jurors to sit in the jury box and pass judgment on Amelia Jenkins, it was the following Monday. It was also time to start the trial for real.

"Ladies and gentlemen of the jury," Judge Kalamaka announced at 9:06 that morning after the jurors had all taken their seats in the jury box, "please give your attention to Mr. Quinlan who will now deliver the opening statement on behalf of the State of Washington."

Quinlan stood up from his seat behind the prosecution table and buttoned his suitcoat. "Thank you, Your Honor. Counsel. Members of the jury. May it please the Court."

A litany of awkward, antiquated phrases that made lawyers feel more important than regular people, without realizing it made regular people think lawyers were jerks who thought they were better than regular people. Quinlan wasn't actually a bad lawyer; he had just developed a lot of bad habits over the years. It wasn't entirely his fault; it was the nature of being a prosecutor. Juries thought you were the good guy, detectives did all your work for you, and almost all of your witnesses were professionals getting paid by the same System as you. It was hard to lose, and if you never lost, you never learned.

So, whatever his natural skills as a lawyer, Quinlan's efficacy as an advocate was undercut by saying things like, 'May it please the Court', right before trying to make a connection with the twelve strangers who would decide whether he won or lost.

Still, they had no choice but to sit and listen to him as he walked over and stopped in front of the jury box, hands spread wide in a gesture they taught you in law school meant 'sincerity'. If that wasn't the pinnacle of lawyering, Talon didn't know what was.

She was also captive to Quinlan's presentation, but at least she wanted to listen. If only to know how to use it against him when she stood up to deliver her own opening statement immediately after him.

Quinlan cleared his throat, and began,

"The Thin Blue Line. The only thing standing between us and anarchy. The men and women who have taken an oath to serve and protect our community, risking their lives every single day to keep our neighborhoods safe, our homes secure, our families protected."

Vomit, Talon thought. But she wasn't about to object to his obvious attempt to play on the passions and prejudices of the jury. She was more than happy to give Quinlan enough rope to hang himself.

"Now, I know," Quinlan continued, "that recently, we've been having a national conversation on the role of the police in protecting our way of life. And that's a good conversation to have.

A fine conversation. There's nothing wrong with discussing ways to improve training and accountability, with reexamining budget priorities, or with making a truly constructive effort to improve the delivery of the vital services our brave men and women in blue dedicate their lives to deliver to the rest of us.

"But," he raised a righteous finger, "we must draw the line at violence against our officers. That must be a line in the sand. A red line. And it was that line," he turned to point back at Amelia, "that the defendant crossed when she chose to assault one of our very own Tacoma Police Department officers in the line of duty."

Talon looked at the jurors to see if any of them were buying what Quinlan was selling. It would have been a great speech at a cop convention. She wasn't sure it was going to go over quite as well with a random sampling of non-cops. Not everyone involved in that 'national conversation' thought of cops as brave and virtuous defenders of the weak and vulnerable. Talon hoped some of those people were on her jury too.

But it was hard to tell just looking at their faces. It was early in the trial. They were still on their best behavior. They weren't tired yet. Tired of sitting in that box day after day, prohibited from speaking, subject to hours upon hours of lawyers droning on, only too happy to hear themselves speak. By the middle of the trial, they'd be fighting not to roll their eyes. By the end of it, they would have stopped fighting and would be actively nodding along with whichever lawyer's closing argument they agreed most with. Talon didn't need them crossing their arms at Quinlan just yet, but she wouldn't have minded it either.

"You will hear from several witnesses in this case," Quinlan continued. "Most importantly, you will hear from Tacoma Police Officer Matthew Connor, the officer who was assaulted by the defendant. You will also hear from two other Tacoma Police officers, Officer Dillon Langley and Officer Arthur Smith, who were there that day and observed both the assault and what led up to it."

Quinlan started to pace as he got to the actual facts of the story. Another thing they taught you in law school—at least if you took a clinical trial advocacy class with a decent adjunct professor with real world experience—was don't pace when you talk to the jury. Pacing is distracting and communicates uncertainty in the information being provided. It was essentially a pacifier for the nervous lawyer. Which begged the question, even if subconsciously, 'Why is this lawyer nervous?' Talon smiled.

"Officer Connor was on routine patrol in what the police refer to as Sector One," Quinlan told the jurors. "Sector One includes the waterfront, all of downtown, and this very building, the courthouse, or more correctly, the County-City Building. That's right, this crime against law enforcement occurred right outside this very building dedicated to the rule of law and protection of the innocent."

In Talon's experience, it was more dedicated to the prosecution of the innocent, but she could make that point later. In her closing argument. When, she hoped, some of those jurors would be nodding along with her.

"While on patrol, Officer Connor came across a vagrant who had passed out in the landscaping in front of the building," Quinlan continued. "The vagrant was a grown man, approximately the same height and weight as Officer Connor. Officer Connor didn't know if the subject would possibly be hostile or might be under the influence of some sort of controlled substance that might make him aggressive or belligerent."

But he assumed all of that, Talon wanted to add.

"So, Officer Connor called for backup and waited for Officers Langley and Smith to arrive before engaging the subject.

Now, it's important to note that the officers were not conducting any sort of criminal investigation. Their charge is to protect and serve. Sometimes that means catching bad guys, but sometimes it means helping people out of public landscaping before they get arrested for trespassing or property damage. That's what was happening here. Just standard, run-of-the-mill community caretaking. Exactly what we want our police officers to do to help keep everyone safe."

Quinlan was still pacing. Every time he reached one end of the jury box, he would pivot and walk slowly back to the other end. Talon found it annoying, but not as annoying as the spin Quinlan was putting on what happened that day in front of the courthouse.

"What happened next was that the defendant," another gesture toward the defense table, although without looking that time, "came upon the officers doing their job to help a citizen, completely misconstrued the situation, obstructed the officers in the discharge of their official duties, then nearly killed Officer Connor by trying to run him over with her car."

All of the jurors turned to look at Amelia. They were each making a personal assessment, right there and then, without having heard any evidence at all yet, whether they thought Amelia, based on her appearance alone, looked like the sort of person who would try to run over a cop with her car. Talon could only hope she didn't. She hadn't gotten to say a word yet, and already opinions were hardening.

"The defendant pulled up next to the officers in her car," Quinlan explained, "blocking the crosswalk and entrance to the courthouse, by the way, and began yelling profanities at the officers, accusing them of police brutality and the like. The officers asked her to move along and tried to explain that she was misunderstanding the situation. But she wouldn't listen. Instead, she continued to berate the officers. At that point, she became a potential safety risk to the officers. They didn't know whether she might attack them physically."

But they assumed she would, Talon thought.

"So, the officers had to stop what they were doing to help the man in the bushes in order to address the threat the defendant was posing to them. They explained that she was obstructing them, which is a crime in and of itself, but the defendant continued to accuse the officers of all sorts of terrible things. Officer Connor asked her to move along and explained forcefully but professionally that if she failed to stop being a threatening presence, they would have no choice but to arrest her for obstructing a law enforcement officer. In response, the defendant took out her phone and said she was going to film them."

Talon wondered whether Quinlan might gloss over that part. Filming cops was a lot different from obstructing them, although the cops would disagree. If being filmed interrupts your official duties, maybe what you were doing wasn't really all that official after all. Talon had hoped he might skip it, so she could bring it up in her opening statement and make the State look like they were hiding something. Quinlan at least didn't make that mistake, but he did the next best thing. He overreached.

"The phone in the defendant's hand was a potential weapon," Quinlan actually had the gall to claim, "and so Officer Connor had no choice but to detain the defendant, at least long enough to ensure the safety of himself and his fellow officers. He informed the defendant she was under arrest and directed her to exit her vehicle. But the defendant refused."

Talon noticed that Quinlan was refusing to use Amelia's name. It was an old prosecutor trick. Dehumanize the defendant by referring to them only as 'the defendant' and never by name. It was dirty pool, but most of them did it, and the judges let them. Talon would just use courtroom judo, and use it against Quinlan as the case proceeded. If the jurors could see her as Amelia instead of just 'the defendant', it would subconsciously undermine Quinlan's entire narrative.

"Officers Langley and Smith had to come over to assist in the detention of the defendant, and in so doing, they had to leave the man who needed their help. The defendant was obviously going to try to drive away, so Officer Connor eventually positioned himself in front of the defendant's vehicle to prevent her escape. When he did so, the defendant had a choice. She could peacefully submit to the officers' authority and allow them to get back to helping her fellow citizen, or she could choose violence." He looked at Amelia again, then back to the jurors. "She chose violence."

How dramatic, Talon thought. The jurors were all looking at them again, so Talon shook her head slightly and rubbed Amelia's arm reassuringly. A gesture of disbelief and solidarity. It showed the jurors that Talon didn't think she was the monster Quinlan was making her out to be.

"The defendant's car raced forward and nearly ran over Officer Connor. He was able to avoid being struck by the vehicle, but just barely. At that point the other officers were done playing. They were able to obtain control over the vehicle and extract the defendant, placing her under arrest for assaulting Officer Connor with a deadly weapon, and with the intent to inflict death or great bodily harm. For, as you will learn, you don't actually have to strike someone in order to assault them. It is also an assault to attempt to injure them, or even put them in reasonable fear that you are going to injure them."

Quinlan was using all the words from the assault in the first degree statute, Talon knew, even if the lawyers weren't allowed to formally cite to the law in their opening statements.

"Thankfully, mercifully, Officer Connor and his fellow officers were not injured that day," Quinlan started his wrap-up, "but they could have been. For police officers, every day could be their last day on the job. That day, it almost was for Officer Connor. And so at the end of the trial, after you've heard the testimony of these three officers, I will stand up again and ask you to return a verdict of guilty to the crime of assault in the first degree. Thank you."

Quinlan's pacing had left him awkwardly at the far end of the jury box to deliver that last line to the jurors. He started to walk back to his starting position, but then turned and made his way back to the prosecution table. Judge Kalamaka waited for Quinlan to sit down and then addressed the jurors again.

"Ladies and gentlemen, now please give your attention to Ms. Winter," he told them, "who will deliver the opening statement on behalf of the defendant."

CHAPTER 31

Talon stood up and followed mostly the same steps as Quinlan. She thanked the judge, but didn't say, 'May it please the Court'. She stepped out from behind the defense table, but not without giving Amelia another encouraging pat on the shoulder. And she took a spot directly in front of the center of the jury box, but she sure as hell wasn't going to pace.

"The police answer to us," Talon began. "They forget that sometimes. They don't like it. So when someone tries to hold them accountable, they get angry. And when a police officer gets angry at you, you are in a lot of trouble. Because all of this," she gestured around the formally appointed courtroom with its fancy state seal and gold-trimmed flags, "the entire system, will come crashing down on your head."

She pointed at Quinlan. "The prosecutors will charge you with whatever the cops say you did. Uncritically. Unthinking. They'll just do whatever they think they're supposed to do to support 'The Thin Blue Line' and 'Our Boys in Blue' and whatever other propaganda names they've invented to distract from the fact that cops don't help people. They arrest people. That guy in the bushes? If he really needed help, he needed the fire department.

They would have helped him. But cops? No, they weren't trying to help some poor man in a medical crisis. They were bullying a homeless man who was a blight on the office building where the county government meets. And Amelia?" A gesture toward her client. "Amelia Jenkins? She saw what was happening and she wanted the cops to know she was watching them. That's why they got angry, and that's why she sits here today charged with a crime she didn't commit."

Talon waited a moment to allow the introduction to sink in, especially that last part about Amelia being innocent. Technically, she might not have to prove her innocence, since she was allegedly presumed innocent, but the jury was going to want to hear Talon say it. A tired defense opening statement simply saying the State wouldn't meet their burden of proof was essentially an admission of guilt. If they were going to acquit Amelia Jenkins, they were going to want to hear from somebody that she was innocent. Talon was that somebody.

"Let me tell you what really happened that day out in front of the courthouse," Talon continued. "A lot of what Mr. Quinlan told you is accurate, but it's not the whole story. And what he did tell you was so wrapped in pro-police propaganda that it's hard to separate the facts from the spin. But that's okay. That's why we have trials, and that's why you hear from both sides before you make up your minds."

A gentle reminder to keep their minds open. Directed particularly to those of the jurors who might have started to feel inclined to convict after hearing just Quinlan's version of events.

"Officers Connor, Langley, and Smith were on duty that day, and they were patrolling the area that included the County-City Building. That much is accurate. And there was a man in distress who was unconscious or semi-conscious in the bushes out in front of the building. That much is also accurate. Everything after that, though, is false."

Talon could have said 'a lie' but she didn't quite have the proof for that yet. She could have said 'inaccurate' but that would have whitewashed the bad intent of the cops in skewing their reports to support felony assault charges against Amelia. 'False' was right in between. It suggested lying without explicitly saying it, and it was more than just a misunderstanding, or people agreeing to disagree.

"The officers were not trying to help that man," she asserted. "If he was in medical distress, the people who would help him were the paramedics from the fire department. As I said, the fire department helps people. Cops arrest people. And that's what was going to happen to the man who dared to pass out at the entrance to the county office building.

"He was also likely to get roughed up a bit," Talon went on, "because he wasn't really in a state to be able to follow directions quickly, if at all. Rather than take a step back and maybe call those paramedics after all, the officers went to the next level of cop confrontation and started yelling at him. When that didn't work immediately, the yelling turned to threats of violence. 'Get up or you will be tased.' Comply or face the consequences. And it was that scene that Amelia drove up to that day."

Talon took a moment to look at Amelia again, doing her best to throw a warm look at her client.

"Imagine what that was like for her," Talon urged. "What that would be like for anyone who cares about the welfare of other human beings. Here was this man, obviously in distress with three large, uniformed, heavily armed police officers yelling at him to do something he obviously was incapable of doing. There was only one direction that was heading, and it wasn't a good one."

Talon paused again. She wanted the jury to imagine what might have happened if Amelia hadn't intervened. Talon was going to paint her as a hero, but the jury needed to understand what evil she had thwarted.

"It's not hard to imagine," she helped them. "There has been a huge increase in private citizens filming questionable conduct by police officers. Conduct that was not properly or accurately described in the officers' official reports. Reports that were false but would have been believed if it weren't for video evidence from a concerned citizen. Concerned, not necessarily about a homeless man who needed medical help, but concerned about what the cops were about to do to him. That's what Amelia Jenkins was doing. And that's why Officer Connor rushed her vehicle and tried to knock her phone out of her hand."

That was a bit different from what Quinlan had told them. She noticed a few of the jury take a moment to look critically at the prosecution table. *Good*. That meant they would be at least open to what she described next.

"Amelia panicked," Talon admitted. "Not only did she have a large, burly, angry police officer sprinting toward her, but she knew he was angry because she had caught him about to unleash that anger on someone else. That's why she had taken her phone out in the first place. She didn't have to wonder whether Officer Connor would be abusive; she had just witnessed it. So, she just reacted and she tried to drive away."

Talon took another beat. She smiled, just a bit and ruefully, and glanced back at Quinlan for a moment. "To hear Mr. Quinlan tell it," she shook her head, "when Amelia started driving away, the officers had already surrounded her car and she made a decision to try to drive over them rather than be arrested. That's what he wanted it to sound like. But that's not what happened. What happened is that she did drive away, successfully, without hitting anyone or even coming close to it. Think about it. Officer Connor was the first to react and he ran straight toward her. The other two officers were caught flat-footed, just standing there as Amelia put down her phone and pulled away from the curb.

"Now, that should have been the end of it. The cops weren't being filmed and there was that man in the bushes, remember, who needed the help they were supposedly offering. But Amelia had challenged them, challenged them with the simple but revolutionary act of documenting what they were actually doing. That enraged Officer Connor and he wasn't about to let it drop. He sprinted after Amelia's car, and Officer Langley decided to join the pursuit."

Again, all new information for the jury. Any time the prosecution left out details, it raised the question of why. Talon wanted the jurors to ask why.

"Amelia made it to the end of the block and made a left turn as fast as she could, but it wasn't quite fast enough. Officer Connor ran out into the road, directly in front of Amelia's car. He would have been hit. He might have even died. But that didn't happen. It didn't happen because Amelia slammed on the brakes to avoid hitting the officer."

Talon raised a hand. "Let me say that again. Officer Connor would have been hit by a car and potentially seriously injured except for the fact that Amelia Jenkins slammed on her brakes to avoid hitting him, even though doing so meant she was ripped out of the car, slammed onto the cement, thrown into jail, and charged with assaulting the very officer whose life she had actually saved."

Talon shook her head again. "That's the national discussion the prosecutor was talking about. For him, it's an abstract exercise to humor but ultimately resist. For my client, Amelia Jenkins, it's more than a discussion. It's her life. And that life is now in your hands."

Talon wanted them to feel the full weight of what they were being asked to be accomplices to.

"At the end of this trial, after you've heard all of the evidence, about all of the people involved in that incident, and what they actually did, you will not believe Amelia Jenkins committed the crime of assault, and I will ask you to return a verdict of not guilty. Thank you."

Talon returned to her seat. Amelia grabbed her arm and thanked her. Talon hoped the jury saw that too.

Opening statements were over, but opening statements were not evidence. They were statements by the lawyers of what they believed the evidence would show. Evidence was the testimony of witnesses, and it was time to hear from them.

"You may call your first witness, Mr. Quinlan," Judge Kalamaka directed.

"Thank you, Your Honor." Quinlan stood to address the judge. "The State calls Officer Matthew Connor to the stand."

CHAPTER 32

Connor marched into the courtroom. He was in full uniform, but it was the short-sleeved one, to show off his unnaturally swollen biceps. He had closely cropped hair and a thick moustache. Quinlan gestured toward the bench and Connor stepped forward to be sworn in by the judge. A few moments later, he was seated on the witness stand and Quinlan began his direct examination.

"Could you please state your name for the record?"

"Matt Connor," he answered, with a smile to the jury. Police officers were trained to deliver their testimony directly to the jurors instead of back to the prosecutor. It was supposed to be more convincing. It was definitely more manipulative.

"How are you employed, sir?" Quinlan continued.

"I'm a police officer with the Tacoma Police Department," Connor answered.

"How long have you been a police officer?"

Again, to the jurors. "I've been a commissioned law enforcement officer for eight years."

"What is your current rank and assignment?" Quinlan asked.

"I am a patrol officer," Connor explained. "I'm assigned to

First Sector."

"First Sector," Quinlan repeated. "Is that also known as Sector One?"

Connor nodded. "That's what the brass calls it. The guys on the street call it First Sector, or just First. I patrol the First."

Ugh. Talon hoped the jurors thought that sounded as douchey as she did.

"What areas are included in Sector One?" Quinlan asked.

"First includes all of downtown," Connor was going to stick with his name for it, "from the waterfront all the way up to MLK where the Hilltop neighborhood starts."

"And as a patrol officer in Sector One," so was Quinlan, apparently, "what do you do exactly?"

"Proactive interdiction of criminal activity," Connor told the jurors. Then he smiled and repeated it using normal words. "I look for bad guys and stop them."

Quinlan nodded. "Do you also respond to calls from central dispatch?"

"Yes, that too," Connor agreed. "Whatever comes up, we deal with it."

"Okay, thank you, Officer Connor," Quinlan said, signaling the end of the first area of his direct examination. "Now, let's talk about the incident that led to the charges in this case. Do you recall being outside this very building regarding an unwanted subject on the grounds of the County-City Building?"

"Yes, I do," Connor told the jurors.

"Was that a callout?" Quinlan asked, "or proactive interdiction?"

Connor grinned at hearing his phrase back at him. "It was a callout. An anonymous caller reported a possibly intoxicated subject passed out in the front landscaping of the County-City Building. I responded and went directly to locate the subject."

"Were you the first officer on scene?" Quinlan asked.

"Yes, I was," Connor answered. "I usually am," he added with a grin.

"Did any other officers arrive?" Quinlan asked.

"Not initially," Connor answered. "When I responded to the call, that would tell other officers in the area that they didn't need to respond."

"Did other officers eventually join you there, though?"

"Yes," Connor agreed. "When I contacted the subject I determined that he was an adult male, likely under the influence of controlled substances, and therefore I would need backup to engage safely with him. I called for backup and waited. Officers Langley and Smith arrived at my location shortly after that."

"What made you believe the subject might be under the influence of alcohol or drugs?" Quinlan asked.

Connor chuckled. "I've been doing this a long time, counselor. I know when someone is tweaking. This guy was definitely out of it."

"What happened after the other officers arrived?" Quinlan proceeded.

"I recontacted the subject," Connor recounted, "to advise him that he couldn't remain lying on the ground in front of the building."

"Was that successful?"

"No. The subject was nonresponsive."

"So, what did you do next?"

"Well, I couldn't just leave him there," Connor explained to the jury, "so I advised him that he needed to follow my commands or he would be placed under arrest for trespassing and obstructing a law enforcement officer."

"Did he respond to that?"

Connor shook his head. "No. He remained nonresponsive."

"What happened next?"

"I unsnapped the holster on my taser and advised the subject that he needed to follow my commands or I would force his compliance."

"Did you end up having to use your taser?" Quinlan asked.

"Um, no," Connor almost seemed disappointed to answer.

"Why not?"

"I was interrupted by another subject."

"Who was that?"

Connor looked past Quinlan and pointed at Amelia. "Her. The defendant."

Talon patted Amelia's arm again, mostly for the jurors, but she expected Amelia didn't mind the reassurance.

"What did the defendant do that interrupted you?"

"Well, as I said, we were on the front lawn, just on the other side of the sidewalk from Tacoma Avenue," Connor explained. "The defendant drove her vehicle right up to the curb and started shouting obscenities at us, accusing us of police brutality, and threatening us."

"What sort of obscenities?" Quinlan asked.

"Oh, you know, the usual stuff," Connor answered. "Fucking pigs, stuff like that. The usual garbage we have to put up with from cop-haters."

"You said she also threatened you?" Quinlan prompted.

"Yes," Connor confirmed, "she did."

"What did she say when she threatened you?"

Connor shrugged. "I don't remember the exact words, but it was something about making us pay for what she thought we were doing to the subject on the ground. Usual 'fuck the police' stuff."

"Was her presence and behavior of concern to you?"

"Oh, definitely," Connor agreed.

"Why was that?"

"Because instead of one potentially dangerous subject, I now had two."

"Couldn't you just ignore her?"

Connor shook his head. "No. That would jeopardize officer safety. If I turned my attention back to the intoxicated trespassing suspect, the other person—the defendant—could have jumped me from behind."

"Was that a real concern to you?" Quinlan asked.

"With the language she was using against us? Absolutely," Connor answered.

"So, what did you do?"

"I ordered her to move on and disengage from the situation."

"Did she comply?"

"No, sir. She did not."

"So what did you do?"

"I had no choice but to break off from the primary subject," Connor answered, "and engage directly with the defendant."

"No choice?" Quinlan questioned.

"She refused my command to move on," Connor explained. "That meant she was remaining on scene and I had to deal with the threat she presented to myself and my fellow officers."

"Okay," Quinlan said. "So, how did you engage with her?"

"I began to walk toward the defendant's vehicle," Connor said. "I advised her that she would be arrested for obstruction if she refused another order to leave."

"How did she respond?" Quinlan asked. "Did she leave?"

"No, sir," Connor answered. "She produced her cellular

phone and began recording me, accusing me of police brutality even though I was still several feet away from her."

"Was it concerning to you that she had a cellular telephone in her hand?"

"Yes, sir, it was."

"Why?"

"Anything in the hand of a hostile subject can be used as a weapon," Connor answered. "At that point, I considered her an armed suspect and I advised her she was under arrest for the crime of obstructing a police officer."

"Did you attempt to place the defendant under arrest?"

"I did, sir, yes," Connor answered.

"What happened when you did that?" Quinlan asked.

Connor turned again and delivered the payoff line to the jury: "She tried to strike me with her vehicle."

Talon nodded slightly. There was the allegation of assault. Connor just left a few things out between telling her she was under arrest and jumping in front of her car, including the fact that he jumped in front of her car. But Talon wasn't worried. That was what cross-examination was for.

"Did she succeed in striking you with her vehicle?" Quinlan asked.

"No, sir." A relieved look to the jurors. "Thankfully not."

"But would you say you were in reasonable apprehension of great bodily harm?" Quinlan followed up.

Talon almost laughed. Not only was the question leading, it used the exact verbiage of the assault in the first degree statute. *'Would you agree the defendant committed the crime of X?' 'Oh yes, absolutely.'*

"Definitely," Connor again told the jurors. "I was in fear of serious bodily injury."

"Reasonable apprehension of great bodily harm?" Quinlan tried to remind him of the right words to use.

"Yes," Connor agreed quickly. "That."

Talon shook her head slightly. She hoped the jury thought it was as ridiculous as she did, but a quick glance at the jury box suggested at least some of them appeared very concerned for the officer's wellbeing. *Damn.*

"What happened next?" Quinlan continued.

"Officer Langley assisted me," Connor answered. "He removed the defendant from her vehicle and she was placed under arrest."

"For obstructing a law enforcement officer?" Quinlan suggested.

"For assaulting a police officer," Connor answered.

"And did that end the interaction with the defendant?"

"We transported her to the jail," Connor explained, "and then that was the end of our interaction with her."

"What about the other guy?"

Connor took a moment, then shook his head blankly. "Who now?"

"The intoxicated subject in the bushes," Quinlan reminded him. "What happened to that subject?"

"Oh, um, I'm not sure," Connor admitted. "I think Smith dealt with him."

Quinlan nodded and took a moment to check his notes. Then he looked up to the judge and announced, "No further questions, Your Honor."

Judge Kalamaka looked down at Talon. "Any cross-examination, Ms. Winter?"

Of course she had cross-examination for the State's key witness/victim. "Yes, Your Honor. Thank you."

Talon stepped out from behind her counsel table and approached the witness stand. There was a natural place for her to stand, where the distance between her and the witness would allow for just enough personal space for both of them to be comfortable. Talon took one step closer than that and began her questioning.

"You didn't want Ms. Jenkins to record you, did you?"

"That wasn't my concern," Connor answered. "I was worried about her belligerent attitude."

"There were other bystanders watching you," Talon reminded him. "You didn't tell any of them to move along."

"They weren't yelling at us," Connor answered.

"And the thing Ms. Jenkins was yelling at you was that she was recording you. She wanted you to know that, right?"

"She wanted to interfere," Connor returned.

"She wanted to protect that man," Talon asserted.

"He didn't need protection," Conner answered.

"But you said he was in distress," Talon pointed out.

"Not from us."

"Not yet," Talon said.

"What's that supposed to mean?" Connor demanded. He leaned forward in his chair, toward her, neck and biceps bulging just a bit. Talon smiled inside. She didn't mind if the jury saw this cop get angry at a few words from a woman.

"Why would you care if you were being recorded?" she continued. "Don't you guys always say people have nothing to fear from the police if you haven't done anything wrong? That's the same for cops and citizens with cell phones, right?"

"Recording us suggests hostility toward the police," Connor tried to explain, through clenched teeth. "Hostility suggests a threat. And threats need to be neutralized."

"Wow. Okay." Talon was more than happy with that

answer. Time to move on. "Let's talk a little bit about exactly where all of this happened." She stepped around the witness stand and extracted the easel and large drawing pad stored there for witnesses to use during their testimony. "Could you please draw a diagram of the scene, including where Ms. Jenkins was when you first observed her and where she was when she was pulled from her car and arrested?"

Connor hesitated. "Uh, I'm not very good at drawing," he claimed.

"Great," Talon responded. "Do it anyway."

Connor grumbled, but then pushed himself out of his seat and pulled a marker off the easel. After a few moments of halting squeaks on the paper, he turned back around. "There."

He had drawn a large rectangle and three Xs.

"What are we looking at here?" Talon had to ask.

Connor pointed at the rectangle. "So, that's the County-City Building. The Xs are where she was when I first saw her, where I was, and where the man in the bushes was."

Talon nodded. "Okay and where did the alleged assault occur?"

Connor took a moment and then waved a circle over pretty much the entire drawing. "Like, around here somewhere."

Talon had to laugh a little. "Can you be more specific?"

"Um, no," Connor answered. "No, I can't. I wasn't focused on the exact location of where things were happening. I was focused on not being assaulted by your client."

Apparently, Talon was going to have to help him remember. She pointed to the far side of the box. "In fact, it was way over here, right?"

"I can't say for sure," Connor insisted.

"Can't or won't?" Talon challenged.

Conner's expression hardened. "I don't understand the question."

So, Talon asked a different one. "Ms. Jenkins tried to drive away, didn't she?"

"Yes, she did," Connor confirmed.

"But you pursued her, right?"

"She wasn't free to go," Connor explained.

"Because she was under arrest for obstructing you?"

"Correct."

"You ran after her car, right?"

"I pursued her on foot."

"How far?"

"I don't recall."

"Pretty far, though, right?"

"I don't recall."

"In fact, she made it all the way to the end of the block and turned onto the side street there, didn't she?"

"Again, counselor, I was trying to detain a person for a crime," Connor said. "She was overtly hostile to the police and she ended up trying to run me over with her car. I don't see why it matters where on this diagram that happened."

"Or maybe you do see why," Talon suggested.

"I don't understand," Connor replied.

"I know, officer," Talon consoled. "Try to keep up. You were not in fact struck by my client's car, correct?"

Connor nodded. "That is correct."

"In fact, she slammed on her brakes to avoid hitting you after you ran out in front of her moving vehicle, isn't that correct?"

"I recall she was going to strike me with her vehicle," Connor maintained, "and I recall Officer Langley removing her from the vehicle. If I wasn't struck and killed, it was thanks to him, not thanks to your client."

Talon crossed her arms. "What happened to the man in the bushes?"

Connor shrugged. "I'm not sure. I had to deal with your client."

"You didn't get to tase him, did you?"

"I did not tase him, no," Connor answered.

"Because of my client's actions," Talon added. "That must have really made you angry."

Connor was about to reply, but it wasn't a question and Talon was done. "No further questions, Your Honor," she declared.

The judge looked again to Quinlan. "Any redirect-examination, Mr. Quinlan?"

Quinlan hesitated, but seemed to decide he better say something. He didn't bother coming out from behind his table though.

"You were not struck by the defendant's vehicle," he said, "but were you afraid you would be?"

Connor nodded then looked to the jury. "Yes, sir."

"And if you had been hit, did you believe you could have been seriously injured or even killed?"

Another heartfelt look to the jurors. "Absolutely."

"No further questions, Your Honor." Quinlan sat down again.

Talon didn't have any recross based on that.

"May this witness be excused?" Judge Kalamaka asked. It was the last thing the judge asked before inviting the next witness to be called. It basically meant the witness had satisfied their subpoena and couldn't be forced to come back without a new one.

"Yes, Your Honor," Quinlan answered.

Talon agreed. "Yes, Your Honor."

Connor stood up, nodded affably to the jurors one last time, and made his way to the exit.

Quinlan stood up to announce his next witness. "The State calls Dillon Langley to the stand."

CHAPTER 33

Dillon Langley was also dressed in full police uniform. His sleeves were long, but it was the same shiny badge and the same bulging gun belt. He even had the same military style fade haircut. Judge Kalamaka swore him in and Quinlan stepped out from behind his table to conduct his direct examination.

It was the same basic introduction. Name, rank, and badge number. Langley was also a patrol officer, also assigned to Sector One ('the First'), and also responded to the County-City Building regarding the man in the bushes. The only difference was that he arrived as backup for Connor after Connor first accepted the call.

"What did you observe when you arrived to assist Officer Connor?" Quinlan asked.

Langley turned to the jury and very intensely delivered his answer to them. "I observed Officer Connor standing over an adult male, approximately twenty-five to thirty-five years old, with a heavy build and soiled clothing."

"What did you do after making your initial observations?"

"I contacted Officer Connor for a situation report," Langley told the jurors. "He stated that the subject was trespassing on city property and was non-compliant with Officer Connor's commands to leave the property."

"Did you observe anything that confirmed Officer Connor's observations?" Quinlan asked.

Again, a full turn to the jurors and a very intense delivery of his answer. Talon suspected it was making at least some of the jurors uncomfortable. "Yes. I observed Officer Connor instruct the subject to stand up and leave the property, and I observed the subject fail to follow that instruction."

"Were any steps taken to help him comply?"

"Officer Connor advised him he would be arrested for obstruction if he did not comply with our orders," Langley answered. "He also advised him that we would use nonlethal compliance measures to force compliance with our commands."

"Nonlethal compliance measures?" Quinlan repeated.

"The taser," Langley explained to the jury. "We would tase him if he didn't get to his feet and leave."

Wow. Talon wasn't sure who was worse, Connor or Langley. Conner was obviously a jackass and a bully, but he seemed to understand that he should pretend like he wasn't. Langley wasn't even trying.

"Did you eventually place the subject under arrest?" Quinlan continued.

"No, sir."

"Why not?"

"We were interrupted by a second subject," Langley explained, "whose behavior required us to turn our attention to her."

"Is that person in the courtroom today?" Quinlan stepped aside so Langley had a clear view of Amelia Jenkins.

"Yes." Langley pointed at Amelia. "That's her."

"And what did she do," Quinlan asked, "that required you

to disengage from the first suspect and focus on her?"

"She was yelling at us to discontinue our interaction with the first subject and she said she was going to record us."

"How did you react to that?"

"Officer Connor advised her she was under arrest for obstruction."

That seemed a little quicker than Connor made it sound.

"Did you eventually arrest her for obstruction?" Quinlan asked.

"We attempted to," Langley told the jurors, "but then she almost struck Officer Connor with her vehicle, so we also arrested her for assault in the first degree."

"Did you interact any further with the original subject?" Quinlan followed up.

"No. Officer Smith attended to him while Officer Connor and I booked the defendant into jail."

Quinlan nodded a few times to himself, mentally checking off the areas he wanted to cover. The second witness didn't have to give as much detail as the first, because the jury had already heard the minutiae. "No further questions, Your Honor."

Quinlan sat down and Talon stood up. She took the same position she had taken with Connor.

"Where did this alleged assault with the vehicle take place?"

"In front of the County-City Building, ma'am." That time, Langley delivered his answer to Talon without looking at the jurors. In fact he was staring intently at her, almost squinting, as if he was trying to spy in advance whatever tricks she was planning to throw at him, because, after all , she was a defense attorney.

"Directly in front of it?" Talon sought to clarify. "Like where the man in the bushes was?"

"I can't say for certain, ma'am," Langley responded. "I know she moved some distance from the original location, but I can't say how far."

"Could it have happened all the way at the end of the block and around the corner?" Talon asked.

"I can't recall, ma'am," Langley claimed. "I was focused on the safety of Officer Connor, not necessarily what street the vehicle was on."

Talon pointed to the easel and paper behind the witness stand. "Could you please draw a diagram of where the assault took place in relation to the County-City Building, Tacoma Avenue, and the side streets at either end of the building?"

Langley looked at the easel and frowned. "No, ma'am."

Talon was taken aback. "No?"

"No," Langley repeated. "I can't say for sure where it took place, so I won't diagram a guess."

Talon cocked her head at him. "You're refusing to draw the diagram I requested?"

"Yes, ma'am," Langley confirmed.

"Huh," Talon said aloud. She'd have to figure out the best way to use that against Quinlan later. "Alright then, let me ask you this. Officer Connor was not struck by Ms. Jenkins's vehicle, correct?"

"That is correct, ma'am."

"Did Officer Connor jump out of the way, or did Ms. Jenkins slam on the brakes?"

Langley thought for a moment, his squinty eyes thinking they'd spotted a trick. "I can't say, ma'am. I was focused on removing the defendant from her vehicle."

"I thought you just said you were focused on Officer Connor's safety?" she reminded him.

"The best way to ensure Officer Connor's safety was to

remove the defendant from her vehicle."

Talon smiled slightly and shook her head at him. "So, you can't say where the alleged assault happened, or even how it happened, but you arrested my client for assault anyway. Is that correct?"

Langley gave her a sharp nod. "That is correct, ma'am."

Talon shook her head again. He'd given her enough to work with. "No further questions."

Judge Kalamaka looked down to the prosecution table. "Any redirect examination, Mr. Quinlan?"

"No, Your Honor," he answered.

"May this witness be excused?"

"Yes, Your Honor," Quinlan said.

"Yes, Your Honor," Talon agreed.

Quinlan stood up to announce his next witness, but the judge cut him off. "It's getting late in the day," he advised the jurors and the attorneys, "and I don't want to start with a witness only to have their testimony interrupted until tomorrow morning. We will adjourn for the day."

The jurors seemed thankful for the respite.

"Please have your witnesses here and ready to go by nine a.m., Mr. Quinlan," the judge told the prosecutor. "Court is adjourned."

CHAPTER 34

Talon just wanted to go back to her office, but when she got to her office, there was a voice mail from Jason Smerk asking her to come to his office to strategize Grainsley's upcoming motions to dismiss and/or delay the trial yet again. Talon might have considered just ignoring it, but the voice mail was actually from the previous week and she'd been ignoring it every evening for days when she got back to her office after court. But they'd adjourned early that day. And the motions were coming up. And she didn't know when she might get another hour or two free during regular business hours.

She logged into her computer and sent an email to Smerk:

Got your voicemail. On my way now. Hope you're there.

~TW

She didn't want to call because the only thing worse than talking with Smerk in person was talking to him on the phone.

The good news was that Smerk was in fact in his office when Talon arrived. That was also the bad news. After a noticeably short wait, the receptionist led her back to Smerk's corner office with the view of Mount Rainier and Commencement Bay.

"Talon," he stood up from his desk to greet her. "How good

of you to get back to me... after eight days. It's nice to feel important."

Talon shrugged and walked over to Smerk's desk. "Yeah, well, I've been busy. There are these things called trials. You should try one sometime. Super fun."

"Despite what you think of civil practitioners," Smerk sneered, "I have tried more than my fair share of trials."

"To juries?" Talon probed.

Smerk pursed his lips for a moment. "Several of them were tried to jury."

Talon sat down in one of the guest chairs opposite Smerk. "This is why we have to push this case to trial, Jason. Grainsley would rather chew his own foot off than go to trial in two weeks."

"I'm not particularly excited about going to trial in two weeks either," Smerk remarked. "It's possible for both of us to be unprepared."

Talon leaned forward onto Smerk's desk. "Do you trust me, Jason?"

Smerk's brow furrowed and he thought for several seconds before answering, "No. No, I do not trust you. I think you're overconfident and reckless and I'm worried you're going to sink this litigation and take my firm with you."

Talon nodded. She supposed she knew he didn't trust her. She just figured he'd be too cowardly to say it to her face. Well, good for him.

"Let's take it one step at a time," she said. "You wanted to strategize over the 12(b)(6) motion to dismiss and the motion to reopen discovery and delay the trial again, right?"

"Strategize might be too collaborative of a word," Smerk replied. "I'd like to ask you to step away and let someone else handle those motions."

Talon was shaken. "Why?" she demanded.

"Why?" Smerk laughed. "You're in trial, Talon. You are actively in the middle of an actual live trial. It took you nine days to respond to a single voice mail."

"Eight days," Talon corrected. "You said it was eight days before."

Smerk shook his head. "Regardless, you are in no place to come in and argue what might be the most important motions in this entire case. Do you even know when the hearing is?"

Damn. She should know that, shouldn't she? It was probably in her calendar, but Smerk would notice if she tried looking in her phone. "Next... week...?"

"Yes, next week," Smerk huffed. "Good guess. Do you know what day?"

"Mon...day?"

Smerk's nostrils flared. "What time?'

So, it was Monday. She was two for two. "Nine a.m.," she said confidently.

"Ha! No!" Smerk slapped his desk triumphantly. "One o'clock. One o'clock in the afternoon next Monday."

Talon nodded. "Yeah, I can make that work. I'll just talk to Judge Kalamaka about a late start after lunch that day. Maybe we can go a little past noon before we take our lunch recess."

"See? See?" Smerk waved his hand at her frantically. "This is what I'm talking about. This is the most important juncture of a very important litigation, and you're still trying to make it fit into the cracks of your criminal case."

"That case is important," Talon defended. "You wouldn't understand."

"Allow me to suggest," Smerk took a deep breath, "that perhaps it is you who's having trouble understanding. Let me try to explain it this way. Why did you accept that new criminal case even though you knew our case was about to need a lot of attention? I'm not criticizing you—well, okay, maybe I am—but really, I just want you to think about that for a moment, and tell me. Why did you take that case?"

Talon considered for a moment. "Because she's innocent."

"And?"

"And she was going to prison for something she didn't do."

"And?"

"And I was the only one who could help her."

Smerk pointed at her. "There it is. Who is the best lawyer for her? You are. It's best for the client if her lawyer is you. And good on you for being that talented of a criminal defense lawyer."

Good on me? Talon frowned at the expression.

"Now, this case," Smerk continued. "My case. The Tribe's case. Why did you volunteer for this case?"

Talon rubbed a hand over her chin. "Well, there were a lot of reasons, actually."

"Such as?" Smerk encouraged.

"It's my tribe."

"And?"

"And Grainsley's firm tried to trick me into representing the yacht club as a token against my own people."

"And?"

Talon had to think for a moment. "I mean, it's bullshit that the Tribe lost all of their waterfront land and now there's some douchey yacht club on it. What the fuck is a yacht club anyway? This is Tacoma, not Monaco."

Smerk nodded along. "Anything else?"

Talon shrugged. "Probably, but I'm getting tired of this game, so why don't you just tell me? I'm going to need to leave soon to get enough rest for trial tomorrow."

Smerk actually laughed at that. "Look, I know you don't think much of me. I'm sure you make fun of my name and my suspenders behind my back."

Talon forgot not to nod.

"But my firm got hired for a reason," he continued. "The same reason the client in your criminal case hired you. You are the best lawyer for her. And my firm is the best lawyer for the Tribe. I'm sure you want what's best for the Tribe, but you may have noticed, you being the best lawyer for them was not one of the reasons you listed for why you wanted to be on this case. And I think the reason you didn't list it is because you know it isn't true."

Talon frowned, but decided to keep listening instead of arguing. At least for the moment.

"I know you're one hell of a litigator," Smerk continued. "One hell of a trial attorney. You had a good reputation when you were still doing civil, and I've only heard even better things now that you're doing criminal. But right now, this case, it might not be what's best for the Tribe. *You* might not be what's best for the Tribe."

Smerk stopped talking then. But Talon didn't stop thinking. He was right. She didn't think much of him. And she did make fun of his name and his suspenders, although she'd do that to his face too. Finally, she spoke.

"I understand why you're saying what you're saying. I understand that you think you're right. But the reason you think you're right is that you don't understand what I'm doing. That isn't your fault. I haven't told you. But I'm telling you this now: the best thing for the Tribe is for me to handle those motions on Monday."

She sighed and glanced around. "Nice office, Jason, but if we're done, I should go. I got a big day tomorrow. Places to be, pigs to roast."

Smerk offered a puzzled frown. "You're going to a pig roast?"

"Cops, Jason." Talon put a hand to her forehead. "I'm going to cross-examine a cop tomorrow. Roast a pig."

Smerk nodded slowly. "Ah. Oh, well, then. Good luck. And um, good talk."

It wasn't a good talk and she didn't need luck. She needed to go home and crash before getting up and eviscerating the next lying sack of shit, Officer Arthur Smith.

CHAPTER 35

Arthur Smith didn't look like a sack of shit, or even a pig. He just looked like another cop, showing up for court in full uniform, trying to use the myths of his profession to bolster his credibility. *Show up in regular street clothes,* Talon thought, *and see if everyone automatically believes everything you say.*

"Do you solemnly swear or affirm," Judge Kalamaka asked Smith as they both raised their right hands, "that you will tell the truth, the whole truth, and nothing but the truth?"

"I do," Smith answered.

Talon didn't believe it for a second. But she had that plan she'd told Amelia about, and a big part of it depended on Smith's testimony. Talon had known she wasn't going to get the cops' personnel files the first time she asked for them. She would have been pleasantly surprised—stunned, really—if she had won, but that wasn't the reason she asked prior to trial. She asked prior to trial so that when she asked again in the middle of trial, Kalamaka might actually say yes. He might even have to say yes.

Her pitch had been that the cops were lying because what they said was different from what Amelia said. Again, that was never going to work. Quinlan was right: that was the dynamic in basically every criminal case. But what if the cops seemed to be lying because they said different things from each other? Connor and Langley had already diverged from each other over a few smaller points, but they also had some pretty suspicious gaps in their memory and/or perception. Two cops with somewhat differing stories of a quickly developing event from a couple months earlier was probably not going to be enough to get those personnel files. But Smith was going to give yet another version. Talon didn't know exactly how it was going to diverge, but she knew it would. Because all three of them were lying. If they were all telling the truth, their stories would line up. But the stories would not line up, ergo they were liars. And if they really did seem like they were lying, Kalamaka would give Talon those personnel files after all.

She just needed to pay attention to where Smith's testimony diverged the most from Connor's and Langley's, and then draw a huge red circle around those places on her cross-examination.

She loved it when a plan came together.

"Please state your name for the record," Quinlan began, ticking off the usual introductory information.

"Arthur Smith."

"I'm employed as a police officer with the Tacoma Police Department."

"I've been a police officer for twelve years."

"I am assigned as a patrol officer in Sector One."

Then Quinlan moved to the incident in question. "Did you have occasion to respond to a call of a person in distress in front of the County-City Building?"

"Yes, I did."

Smith wasn't looking at the jury when he answered. He delivered his answers back to Quinlan in a way that was very natural, but not what Talon knew he'd been trained to do.

"How did you come to respond to that call?" Quinlan asked.

"Officer Connor had responded to the call originally," Smith explained. "A few minutes later, he called for backup and so I responded to assist him."

"What did you see when you arrived?"

It was the same thing Connor and Langley had described, but the words were slightly different. "There was a gentleman lying in the bushes that form part of the landscaping near the front entrance of the building. He appeared to be in some sort of medical distress. Officer Conner was directing him to stand up and leave the area, but he appeared unable to comply with those commands."

Gentleman. Medical distress. Unable to comply.

Talon was liking Officer Smith so far, despite his uniform.

"What did you do?" Quinlan asked.

"I took up a support position behind Officer Connor," Smith explained. "Officer Langley had begun to engage with the gentleman as well. I didn't believe it would be helpful to the situation to have a third officer directly involved."

"Did the subject ever comply with Officer Connor's or Officer Langley's directives?" Quinlan asked.

"He did not," Smith confirmed.

"Was he advised that continued refusal could lead to his arrest for obstructing a law enforcement officer?"

Smith hesitated. He seemed to be choosing his words before responding. "Officer Connor stated that he would use compliance techniques if the gentleman did not begin to follow his orders."

Like a taser, Talon recalled. Connor had had no qualms about admitting that on the stand.

"Were those increased compliance techniques ever employed?" Quinlan asked.

"No, they were not," Smith seemed relieved to report.

"Why not?" Quinlan asked. "Did he begin to comply?"

"No, he did not," Smith answered. "Officers Connor and Langley were interrupted."

"By what?" Quinlan asked. "Or whom?"

Smith nodded slightly at Amelia. "By the defendant," he answered.

Quinlan turned and pointed. "Officers Connor and Langley's efforts to engage with the man in the bushes were interrupted by the defendant, Amelia Jenkins? Is that correct?"

Just in case the jury didn't catch what Smith had literally just said. Talon rolled her eyes slightly. She knew the jury would be looking at their table, but she was okay with them seeing her begin to grow impatient. She hoped it would mirror what at least some of them were starting to feel.

"Correct," Smith confirmed.

"What did she do to interrupt them?"

Smith considered for a moment. "She pulled her car up to the curb nearest us and yelled, 'Don't hurt that poor homeless man!'"

Quinlan waited for more, but when none came, he asked, "Did she use any profanity?"

Smith twisted his mouth slightly in thought. "She did eventually, I believe. I'm not sure if she did at first."

"Okay, so, eventually she used profanity," Quinlan emphasized that part of the answer. "And did she say anything bad about the police?"

"The police generally?" Smith asked. "No, I don't think so. She just yelled at us to not hurt the man on the ground. She seemed to be concerned for his safety."

"Because he was passed out?" Quinlan suggested.

Smith shook his head. "No. Because he had three cops standing around him."

Talon had stopped taking notes and was watching Officer Smith intently. Not only was his testimony far less damning to Amelia, he also seemed the most credible of the three officers. Although, Talon knew, that might have just been because she wanted to believe him over the other two. She rested her chin on her hand as the examination continued.

"Um, okay," Quinlan stammered. "So, this yelling at you, you said that interrupted what you were doing, correct?"

"It interrupted what Officers Connor and Langley were doing," Smith answered. "I maintained my support position."

"What did the other officers do in response to the interruption?" Quinlan asked.

"Officer Connor ordered her to move along."

"Did she comply?"

"No."

"What did she do?"

"She took out her cell phone and started filming us," Smith said.

"What happened next?"

"Officer Connor broke of his contact with the gentleman in the bushes and moved quickly toward the defendant's vehicle," Smith answered. "Officer Langley followed him."

"What did you do?"

"I stayed with the man in the bushes."

"Did Officer Connor say anything to the defendant as he approached her vehicle?" Quinlan continued.

"He ordered her to stop filming or she would be arrested for obstruction," Smith said.

"Did she stop?"

Smith thought for a moment. "Yes, she did."

That seemed to throw Quinlan for a moment. "She did?"

"Yes," Smith explained, "because she started to drive away."

"Ah." Quinlan relaxed. "And that was when she almost struck Officer Connor with her vehicle, correct?"

Smith didn't answer immediately. He frowned and shifted his weight on the witness stand. Finally he said, "I don't believe I saw that happen."

That was interesting, Talon thought. *What did he mean by that exactly?*

"Why not?" Quinlan asked before he realized he shouldn't. Then, he amended his question to suggest its answer. "Is it because your attention was on the gentleman in the bushes?"

Smith took a moment again and then nodded. "That was part of it."

Quinlan took a moment then. Several of them. He had undoubtedly scripted out all of the questions he was going to ask Smith, but he suddenly seemed less than confident about the answers he might receive.

"In fact," he said finally, "you were left to deal with the man in the bushes yourself, isn't that correct?"

Smith nodded. "Yes, sir."

"What did you do?" Quinlan asked. "How did that resolve? Was he arrested for trespassing?"

"No, sir." Smith shook his head. "I determined that he was likely undergoing some sort of acute mental health episode. I contacted dispatch for a Designated Crisis Responder to come to the scene and evaluate him."

For the first time in his testimony, Smith turned to the jury to explain, "A Designated Crisis Responder is a trained mental health professional who contacts people who might be undergoing a mental health crisis. They aren't police officers. They determine whether the person is in need of emergency mental health services and, if so, they can temporarily commit the person for up to seventy-two hours at a local mental health facility for assessment and treatment."

Quinlan blinked at the answer, but he must have decided he needed to follow up. "Was the man committed?"

Smith nodded. "Yes, sir. He was having an acute episode. The D.C.R. put a hold on him and he was transported to Tacoma General Hospital to get the help he needed."

Quinlan seemed disappointed in that resolution to the interaction with the man in the bushes. He hurried to end the examination. "So, you had no further interaction with the defendant, is that correct?"

"That is correct, sir." Smith seemed relieved as well to end the questioning from the prosecutor.

Quinlan announced, "No further questions!" and it was Talon's turn.

She too had a script of questions she planned to ask Smith. But like she had told Charlotte Draper in their first meeting, trial work was fluid and dynamic. Anything could happen, and usually did. Talon came into the trial with a plan. But plans change. She thought maybe she had a better plan.

"Thank you, Your Honor," she responded to Judge Kalamaka's invitation to cross-examine Officer Smith.

She stood up and approached the bailiff, and the exhibits laid out on the bar in front of him. She picked up the diagram Connor had drawn. It had been collected by the bailiff and folded into a manageable size. Talon unfolded it into a far less manageable sheet of creased paper and stood where both Smith and the jurors could see it.

"Officer Smith, if someone said that the interaction where Ms. Jenkins was pulled from her vehicle by Officer Langley happened right here," she pointed at the spot on the diagram near the entrance to the courthouse and the gentleman in the bushes, "would that be accurate?"

Smith shook his head. "No, ma'am."

"And if someone said it happened over here," Talon pointed to the end of the block and around the corner, "would that be accurate?"

Smith nodded. "Yes, ma'am."

Talon nodded as well. She pointed back to the original location she had indicated. "You were back here, correct?"

"Correct."

"You didn't see Ms. Jenkins try to assault Officer Connor way over here, did you?"

Smith took another moment before confirming, "No, ma'am."

There was a common mistake trial lawyers made. It was called, 'asking one question too many'. Talon didn't make that mistake. She had a new plan. She could ask that question later.

"No further questions," she told the judge. She folded up the exhibit again and set it back on the bar before returning to her seat.

"Any redirect-examination, Mr. Quinlan?" Kalamaka asked.

Talon wondered whether Quinlan would risk it. Another common mistake trial lawyers were counseled against was, 'don't ask a question you don't already know the answer to'.

"No, Your Honor," Quinlan said.

Smart man, Talon thought. *But it won't matter.*

"May this witness be excused?" Judge Kalamaka asked.

"Yes, Your Honor," Quinlan seemed relieved to say.

But Talon wasn't about to provide him that relief. "No, Your

Honor," she answered. "We would ask that Officer Smith remain subject to recall."

Smith looked up at the judge for clarification. Quinlan sat down audibly. And Judge Kalamaka explained, "That means you are still under oath and must return to the courtroom for further testimony if requested to do so by either party. Do you understand what that means?"

Smith grimaced slightly. "Yes, Your Honor."

Talon was pretty sure everyone understood what it meant too. Not that any of them could do anything about it.

CHAPTER 36

Before Talon could execute Plan B on the criminal case—or as she preferred to think of it, Plan A-plus—she had to defend the civil case against Grainsley's Plans D and E, having already failed on at least three previous occasions to dodge and delay the impending trial Talon was forcing on him. Testimony in the criminal trial was a bit ahead of schedule thanks to her limited cross-examination of Smith, so Judge Kalamaka agreed to a later start on the Monday afternoon that Talon needed to be in Judge Masters's courtroom down the hall.

She had one hour.

When she arrived at Masters's courtroom, Talon had expected to see an essentially empty courtroom, with just her and Grainsley battling before the judge and her staff, but Smerk and Draper had both also come to observe. And give her advice. She hated it when people gave her advice.

"Are you sure you're ready for this, Talon?" Draper asked.

Smerk's nervous expression showed he was thinking the same thing, but he didn't say anything. He just added an expectant nod to punctuate Draper's question.

"I'm ready," Talon assured them. She didn't feel a need to say more than that assurance.

"Have you thought about the order you want to handle the motions?" Draper asked. "I was thinking, maybe if you do the motion to delay the trial date first, and she does delay it, then we could ask to also delay the dismissal motion."

To confirm, that would work, Grainsley interjected himself into the conversation from his seat at the defense table.

"I would be willing to strike the 12(b)(6) motion entirely," he offered, "if we can agree to delay the trial date and restart normal discovery."

"Normal, meaning you refuse to answer our interrogatories?" Smerk challenged.

Good on you, Jason, Talon thought.

Grainsley smiled as well, a meaty, twisted thing. "I can agree to be less obstructionist if you can agree to extending the trial date."

"Sorry, nope," Talon finally put in. "We're going to argue the 12(b)(6) motion first. I'm going to win that. Then I'm going to win the motion to delay everything forever. Then we're going to be back here in a week, and I'm going to win the trial. That's the plan. End of discussion."

Grainsley narrowed his puffy eyes at her, then looked to Draper. "You're the client," he told her. "You make the decisions."

"She's my client," Talon returned, "and you don't ever talk to her directly again or I file a bar complaint against you for knowingly communicating with a represented person. Understood, Peter?"

Grainsley definitely understood. The Rules of Professional Conduct specifically prohibited lawyers from talking directly to other lawyers' clients. It only made sense, otherwise they would constantly be pulling the kind of stuff Grainsley just tried. He grunted and turned back to the notepad on his table. "We'll see about all that," he muttered. "We'll see."

Draper looked like she was about to argue the point with Talon. She could, in fact, tell Talon to accept Grainsley's proposal. Grainsley was right about that—the client made the decisions. But Talon warned her off with a shake of her head. "Don't second-guess me," she reminded her.

Draper thought for a moment, then nodded. "Good luck."

She and Smerk retreated to the gallery and a few minutes later Judge Masters took the bench. After the call of the bailiff to 'all rise' and the direction of the judge to 'be seated', they were ready to begin.

"We have two motions scheduled for this afternoon," Judge Masters began. "Do the parties have any preference as to which—?"

"We would ask to address the 12(b)(6) motion to dismiss first, Your Honor," Talon jumped in. "It's a dispositive motion, so it only makes sense to handle it before scheduling matters that would become moot if the case is dismissed."

Masters nodded. "That does seem to make sense. Do you agree, Mr. Grainsley?"

Grainsley stood up, slowly, to address the judge. "I attempted to discuss the order of these motions with Ms. Winter prior to the Court taking the bench, but those discussions proved fruitless. I would defer to the wisdom of the Court, Your Honor."

Masters frowned slightly at the extra information, but accepted his position, or lack thereof, as to the order of the motions. "All right then, we will begin with defendant's motion to dismiss under Civil Rule 12(b)(6). This is your motion, Mr. Grainsley—actually, they both are—so I shall hear first from you."

Grainsley was still standing. He knew he'd be speaking first regardless of the order of motions, and raising and lowering that body of his was no easy task.

"Thank you, Your Honor," he began. "Defendant Commencement Bay Yacht Club brings this motion to dismiss under Civil Rule 12(b)(6) which states, in pertinent part, that the Court may dismiss a cause of action for 'failure to state a claim upon which relief can be granted'. In this case, plaintiff Puyallup Tribe of Indians has failed to state a claim upon which relief can be granted. Specifically, they have failed to allege any facts which, if true, would lead to the remedy they seek, to wit: the seizure and transfer of real property belonging to the yacht club over to the Tribe. Therefore, the Court should avoid the waste of judicial resources that would accompany a trial they legally cannot win and dismiss the case."

Grainsley took a breath. A large loud breath. He seemed more tired than at their previous hearings. Talon wondered about his health. Not out of concern, but strategy.

"I should point out, Your Honor, that I would normally have filed a motion for summary judgment," Grainsley continued, "which would have the same result of a dismissal. However, a motion for summary judgment is usually reserved for after discovery is complete and it is still my position that discovery in this matter is woefully incomplete, despite the Court's orders regarding the scheduling of the trial."

Talon winced. It was never a good idea to poke the judge in the eye when you were asking her to rule for you. Especially when you were asking for the most extreme remedy possible.

Masters acknowledged the dig with a slight frown and even slighter nod. "Continue, Mr. Grainsley," she instructed.

"Of course, Your Honor," Grainsley said. "I only wished the Court to understand our complete position. This motion to dismiss could be avoided and handled more properly later as a summary judgment motion if the Court were to decide to delay the trial date and allow further discovery. I think the Court should have that in mind when making its rulings."

Masters didn't say anything. Which said a lot.

Grainsley continued. "In any event, the Court should dismiss this case because the land in question has belonged to the yacht club since its inception in 1912. Although it wasn't fully developed into the restaurant and hotel complex that now sits on it until relatively recently, there has never been a question as to its proper title. Indeed, it is the added value of the new complex which seems to be the motivation behind this litigation. When it sat as an empty lot, used as storage for cleaning and construction supplies, the Tribe apparently had no interest in it. Now that it houses a successful business, suddenly it is Tribal land and must be returned to the Tribe. The only problem, Your Honor, is that it cannot be returned because it was never theirs. Not legally, and not in any way that should matter to the courts of the State of Washington."

There it is, Talon thought. The only shade of an acknowledgment that the land in question, hotel or not, was in fact once a part of the land of the Tribe, before it was taken away by the governments of the United States and the State of Washington. The same governments whose courts would decide its ownership now. That hardly seemed fair, because it wasn't. And Grainsley was counting on that.

"I won't go into a lengthy recitation of the laws that have addressed the proper title of the land in and around the Port of Tacoma," Grainsley went on. "This isn't a case about fishing rights or modes of self-governance. This isn't even really a case about the boundaries of the Tribe's reservation. It is quite simply, Your Honor, a case about greed and an unabashed land grab to profit off the hard work and success of others. An effort hoping to wrap itself in larger societal movements claiming to promote social justice and equality, while truly having nothing to do with either."

Was he really going to make this about money? Talon wondered.

"The Puyallup Tribe of Indians has become a very successful entity, Your Honor," Grainsley leaned into it. "Their casino and resort complex has flourished, doubling or maybe even tripling in size from the days of a single building on the side of Interstate-Five. Apparently, however, their appetite to control the entertainment venues south and east of downtown Tacoma cannot be sated. They saw the success of the yacht club's restaurant and they felt entitled to own that success as well. If the club had left it a storage yard, you can be sure this litigation would never have been brought. But my client dared to improve and invest, and now the Tribe dares to try to take it away.

"But the Court can and should prevent that. The Court can and should see this litigation for what it really is: a baseless land grab with no support in the facts or the law. The plaintiff has failed to state a claim upon which relief can be granted. Accordingly, the Court can and should dismiss this case. Thank you."

He sat down again hurriedly, almost falling into his seat. His face wasn't red, but he was sweating at the temples. Talon wondered whether he believed a word of what he had just argued. But she also knew it didn't matter. He'd argued it anyway.

"Thank you, Mr. Grainsley," Masters said. She turned to the plaintiff's counsel table. "Response, Ms. Winter?"

Talon stood up. "Thank you, Your Honor. As tempted as I am to respond to the underlying implications regarding the motivations of my client in bringing this litigation, I will stick to the law, and the facts, because it is the combination of those two things which lead to the inescapable conclusion that not only has the Tribe absolutely stated a claim upon which relief can be granted, but that relief is the only reasonable conclusion to this litigation and will certainly be the verdict of any jury after hearing the evidence at trial. The Court should therefore deny the defendant's motion to dismiss and allow the case to proceed to that trial and that jury."

Talon moved from dramatic opening to logical presentation.

"The land in question, Your Honor, was part of the land historically associated with the Puyallup Tribe of Indians prior to arrival of the first White settlers at Puget Sound. When those settlers arrived, conflicts arose regarding the ownership and use of land and other natural resources in the area. Eventually, on December 26, 1854, the Medicine Creek Treaty was entered into between the United States government and over sixty local native tribes, including the Puyallup Tribe. It goes almost without saying that the treaty was entered into under the duress of the burgeoning colonialism of the settlers, and it also goes almost without saying that those same settlers and same United States government almost immediately began violating both the letter and the spirit of the treaty.

"Despite guarantees not only for actual land for their people, but also rights to fish and otherwise have access to the resources of the area, laws were passed to restrict that land and those rights. Efforts by the Tribe and its allies to assert those rights were met with force and further oppression, including the well-publicized arrest of Marlon Brando in the 1960s for daring to go fishing with Robert Satiacum, the then-leader of the Tribe. The Tribe dared to assert the rights it had treated for and was rewarded with further subjugation and arrest. But the Tribe would not give up the fight. In fact, they took the fight to the courts. And they won.

"A series of legal victories in state and federal court

eventually gave the Tribe sufficient bargaining power to secure the Puyallup Lands Claim Settlement in 1990. As part of that settlement, lands that had been *de facto* taken from the Tribe despite being *de jure* secured to them in the Medicine Creek Treaty were to be returned to the Tribe. Many of those tracts of land had already been developed by non-Tribal members and entities and so a procedure was established for the fair and appropriate transfer of those lands back to the Tribe. One such parcel is the land upon which the Commencement Bay Yacht Club built its restaurant and hotel."

Talon took a moment to assess how her history lesson was going over. Grainsley was frowning. That was good. Masters was still listening. That was also good. She pressed ahead.

"The Tribe is now asserting its title to that land," she said. "Mr. Grainsley brings this motion to dismiss, alleging the Tribe has failed to state a claim upon which relief can be granted, but in doing so he inadvertently reveals that the Tribe has stated a claim upon which relief *must* be granted. The legal standard for deciding a motion like this is that the Court assumes the truth of the Tribe's claims, draws any and all reasonable inferences in favor of the Tribe, and then decides whether any reasonable jury could decide in favor of the Tribe. If there are in fact any facts in dispute, then the motion also fails, because the jury is the only proper entity to decide disputes as to facts. Here, in this case, not only are there no disputes as to the facts, but no reasonable jury could decide in favor of anyone but the Tribe."

She raised her hands and ticked off the facts not in dispute. "This land was part of the historical land of the Puyallup Tribe. This land was guaranteed to the Tribe in the Medicine Creek Treaty. This land was again guaranteed to the Tribe in the Puyallup Lands Claim Settlement. That restaurant and that hotel change those facts not one iota. Ignoring the law does not change the law. The yacht club can ignore the law, but this Court cannot. It should not. And, I am confident, Your Honor, it will not. Deny the motion to dismiss and let this case proceed to the trial it deserves and the victory the Tribe will win. Thank you."

Talon sat down again. She wasn't sweating at the temples. She was happy with her argument. She considered turning around to see if Draper and Smerk were equally pleased, but that would have seemed needy. Besides, she wanted to focus on the judge's ruling.

"Thank you, counsel," Judge Masters began. "Both counsel, I mean. I appreciate the arguments made on both sides, and I appreciate the importance of this case to both parties. There is a significant economic interest to the defendant Commencement Bay Yacht Club, and there is a significant historical interest to the plaintiff Puyallup Tribe of Indians. These interests are at odds, at least partially, and are sufficiently intertwined as to resist a simple resolution that would satisfy both parties, or maybe even either party."

The judge frowned and nodded to herself as she began to deliver her next words. "It is for that very reason that I hesitate to grant any motion that would settle this matter without a complete airing of all the interests and arguments on both sides. The defendant is asking me to terminate this case right here and right now on an assertion that they cannot possibly lose. The plaintiff is asking me to deny the motion and makes a similar argument that they cannot possibly lose at trial either. And while I appreciate the confidence of the attorneys, they can't both be right. In fact, they are probably both wrong. But if I can see one of them being closer to right, that they cannot lose on the facts and the law as argued here, I would have to say that Ms. Winter presents the stronger case."

Talon allowed a small smile. She was going to win the motion. She might even get something extra from the judge.

"Assuming the truth of the Tribe's claim," Judge Masters made her ruling, "and drawing all reasonable inferences in favor of the Tribe, I cannot say they could not win this case. Therefore I am going to deny the motion to dismiss under Rule 12(b)(6)."

Talon's smile broadened. Then it broadened even more as Masters continued.

"Part of the reason I agreed to Ms. Winter's proposal of an accelerated trial schedule," the judge said, "and part of the reason I am very unlikely to grant any motion to delay the trial or reopen discovery, was my belief that this case will be decided primarily on the history of the legal status of the land in question, and far less so on the specific facts of how the land has been or will be used."

Judge Masters looked at the clock on the courtroom wall. So did Talon.

"We have been in session for almost an hour now," the judge observed. "I think the parties know how I am going to rule on the motion to continue the trial date. Perhaps we should take a recess now for the parties to consider their respective positions. There is often a landing space between total victory and total defeat. I would urge the parties to try, earnestly, to find that space now, lest one side or the other receive that total defeat from the jury."

Judge Masters paused for a moment, then added. "Does that make sense, Mr. Grainsley?"

The judge's failure to include Talon in her admonition made the point crystal clear, even to Grainsley. He pushed himself to his feet. "Yes, Your Honor," he answered humbly.

"Good," Masters said. She lifted the gavel in front of her and held it over its strike plate. "Court will be at recess. Advise me when there's been a breakthrough."

The judge pounded her gavel and retreated to her chambers, with her bailiff and court reporter in tow. Smerk and Draper came forward to where Talon was standing. Then Grainsley stepped over to the three of them. "Apparently," he sighed, "we should talk."

Talon loved it when the other side blinked.

"My work here is done," she declared. "Jason can and should take it from here. I have another matter to attend to anyway."

"Thank you, Talon," Draper said. "You were right."

Not to second-guess her, went unspoken.

Talon nodded in acknowledgement. "I know."

Now, to make her other opponent blink.

CHAPTER 37

The main difference between Peter Grainsley and Eric Quinlan was that Grainsley was smart. Not that Quinlan was entirely stupid, but Talon wasn't sure he would be as quick to appreciate that he'd lost. It would take more than a telling eyebrow from a judge for him to realize he would lose. He would need to be convinced that he *should* lose. And even then, Talon didn't trust him to do the ethical thing. Plan A-plus might require a Plan A-plus-two. But she was ready with that too, if need be.

Talon hurried into Kalamaka's court to find the stage perfectly set. Amelia had already been transported and was waiting at the defense table. Quinlan was seated at the prosecution table looking as oblivious as ever. The court reporter was at her station, and the bailiff looked up expectantly at her entrance, ready to summon the judge and jury so they could proceed.

And proceed they could, because the final stage prop was also present. Officer Arthur Smith sat in the back row of the courtroom, again in full uniform, again ready to testify.

"Thank you for coming," Talon said to him.

He shrugged. "I wasn't excused," he recalled, "and you told me to be here."

"I'm not sure that would have been enough for everyone," Talon replied. She avoided saying 'every cop', even though they both knew that's what she meant.

"It's enough for me," Smith answered.

And that's why Talon had switched to Plan A-plus.

She strode down to her spot next to her client and informed the bailiff that she was ready to proceed. The bailiff fetched the judge, and then brought out the jurors. It was time for Talon's case-in-chief.

After Smith's testimony, Quinlan had filled the rest of his own case with the other minor witnesses needed to put everything in perspective. The characters at the beginning and end of the story who helped spread the narrative to a complete arc. The county employee who had first seen the man in the bushes. The other employee who called 9-1-1. The cops who towed away Amelia's car and impounded it, at her still ongoing expense, Talon pointed out on cross-examination. But the case really boiled down to the testimony of the people directly involved in the incident.

Officer Connor. Officer Langley. Officer Smith.

And Amelia Jenkins.

"The defense may call its first witness," Judge Kalamaka declared.

Talon stood. "The defense calls Amelia Jenkins to the stand."

It wasn't always the right decision to put your criminal defendant client on the stand. In fact, it usually wasn't. For one thing, they were often guilty, and it was rare that putting a guilty client on the stand to admit they were guilty would lead to an acquittal. For another, even if they were innocent, they would be nervous, and that could look suspicious on its own. Throw in an effective cross-examination by a talented prosecutor and even an innocent client could sink themselves. On the other hand, juries really wanted to hear a defendant tell them they didn't do it. And Quinlan was not a talented prosecutor.

Amelia walked up to be sworn in by the judge. Although she was in custody, the jury wasn't allowed to know that. They might conclude, reasonably, that the judge must think she was guilty if he was holding her in jail pending the formality of a verdict. So, for the entire trial, Amelia had been brought to court in street clothes, appropriate for court, and had her handcuffs removed prior to the jurors emerging into the courtroom from their jury room. The only suggestion that Amelia was not free to leave with everyone else at the end of the day were the guards stationed at the exits, but the jurors were left to conclude they were just extra security.

"Do you swear to tell the truth, the whole truth, and nothing but the truth?" Kalamaka asked her, hand raised.

"I do," Amelia answered, hand also raised. Then she stepped to the witness stand, sat down, and waited for Talon to ask her first question.

That first question was her name, followed by some basic background. Her age, how long she had lived in Tacoma, family members, place of employment. The jury didn't need to know everything about her, but they needed to feel like she was a real person.

"Let's talk about the event that led to the case here," Talon indicated a transition to the next area of testimony. It was for both Amelia and the jurors. She wanted them all to be paying attention, and sometimes pointing out the sights was the best way to make sure they were seen.

"Tell the jury how you happened to come across the incident taking place in front of the County-City Building that day."

So, she did. It was the same thing Talon had observed

herself firsthand. Amelia was driving by on her way somewhere else when she saw three large, uniformed, armed police officers standing over a homeless man on the ground. She drove up and yelled at them not to hurt him. She told them she was going to film them. One of them ran at her. She got scared and tried to drive away. They ran after her. She turned left on the next street. One of the cops jumped in front of her car. She slammed on her brakes so she wouldn't hit him. She didn't hit him. She got yanked out of her car and slammed on the ground. They handcuffed her. They told her she was under arrest for assaulting a police officer. They left her car there and booked her into jail. And now she was on trial for an assault that she didn't commit.

"At any time," got to the heart of the case, "did you intend to inflict great bodily harm on Officer Connor?"

"No."

Not Assault One.

Amelia had delivered all of her answers to Talon, not the jury. That was part of the plan too. It seemed more authentic, and Talon wanted the jurors to find her authentic. Credible. Believable.

"Did you intend to strike Officer Connor with your vehicle?"

"No."

Not Assault Two.

"Did you intend to create in Officer Connor apprehension and fear of bodily injury, even if you did not intend to actually cause bodily injury?"

"No."

Not assault at all.

"Thank you, Ms. Jenkins," Talon concluded. "No further questions."

If only Amelia could have gone back to the defense table

with Talon, but when she took the stand, she was like any other witness, and witnesses were cross-examined.

"Any cross-examination, Mr. Quinlan?" Judge Kalamaka asked.

Quinlan could have said no, of course. He didn't have to cross-examine any witness. Neither of them did. But some witnesses couldn't be allowed to testify unchallenged. Talon couldn't not cross Matt Connor. And Quinlan couldn't not cross Amelia Jenkins.

The good news was that most prosecutors weren't very good at cross-examination. They didn't get a lot of practice. Most defendants chose not to testify, and a lot of times, the defense put on no witnesses at all—they just argued that the State's evidence didn't meet the standard of proof beyond a reasonable doubt.

The best cross-examination was usually short and sweet, surgical, exploiting and exposing the weaknesses in the witness's testimony, then sitting down again. It took time to learn how to do that, and even more time to trust yourself doing it. A lot of younger defense attorneys made the rookie mistake of starting from the top and taking the witness through everything they had already said again, letting them testify twice. Rookie defense attorneys and unpracticed prosecutors.

"So, you say you saw three police officers harassing a homeless man?" Quinlan began, just in case the jury had forgotten Amelia's honorable motives.

"Yes," Amelia confirmed.

"And you claim you were worried for the man's safety, is that correct?" Quinlan allowed her to say it twice.

"Yes, that's correct."

And so it went. Amelia was able to tell the jurors a second time, through Quinlan, that she was afraid for the man's safety, that she never got out of her car or otherwise actually interfered with what they were doing, that she only told the police she was filming them, that her saying that set off Officer Connor, that he ran at her full speed yelling that she was under arrest for obstruction, and that she was so scared she sped away.

"So, you did not submit to his order that you were under arrest?" Quinlan tried to build an '*a-ha!*' moment out of all that.

"I was scared, sir," Amelia explained. "I saw how they were treating that poor man, and I saw how angry that policeman was. I was afraid I would get hurt, so I just reacted and tried to get away."

Talon stole a look at the jurors. A few of them were nodding. Most of them were leaning forward. None of them had crossed arms. *Good. All good.*

"Officer Connor positioned himself in front of your vehicle, did he not?" Quinlan asked.

"He jumped in front of it." Amelia nodded. "Yes, sir."

"He tried to keep you from leaving," Quinlan argued, "after telling you that you were under arrest, correct?"

Amelia shrugged. "I suppose so."

"And you nearly struck him with your vehicle," Quinlan asserted, "which would undoubtedly have caused great bodily harm."

Not a question, but Talon didn't object. Amelia was handling him fine. And anyway, it wasn't really about what Amelia said anymore. Not directly.

"I slammed on my brakes," Amelia answered.

"You were removed from your vehicle by Officer Langley," Quinlan countered, suggesting that was the real reason she hadn't struck Connor.

"Yes, sir," Amelia answered the question, but not Quinlan's implication.

Quinlan raised his chin triumphantly. "No further questions,

Your Honor."

Normally Talon would have done some redirect-examination, if only to dispel some of those unfair implications Quinlan had thrown around. But she wanted to get to the next witness.

"Any redirect-examination, Ms. Winter?" Judge Kalamaka asked.

"No, Your Honor," she answered.

That ended Amelia's time on the stand. There would be no question about whether she was excused. She was in custody, so she definitely wasn't excused in the traditional sense, but as a criminal defendant with the right to remain silent, Quinlan couldn't call her as a witness. When she finished testifying, as had just happened, she was done without any further inquiry from the judge, fully excused from being recalled to the stand. Unlike Talon's next witness.

"The defense recalls Officer Arthur Smith to the stand," Talon announced as Amelia sat down next to her.

It was a dramatic moment. A defense attorney calling a cop to the stand? It seemed risky. And it was. But fortune favors the bold. Risks were part of trial work. That was why Grainsley had finally blinked.

"You are still under oath," Judge Kalamaka reminded Officer Smith as he retook the witness stand.

Smith acknowledged that fact and sat down.

Part of why Talon felt the risk of calling a cop in her case-in-chief was acceptable was that she believed he would tell the truth. The other part was that she only had three questions for him.

"You just listened to all of Ms. Jenkins's testimony just now, didn't you?"

Smith nodded. "Yes, ma'am, I did."

"Every single thing she said was true, wasn't it?"

Another nod. "Yes, ma'am, it was."

"And if anyone testified differently from what Amelia Jenkins said, that wouldn't be true, would it?"

A sigh. Then an answer. "No, ma'am. It would not."

"No further questions."

Talon marched back to her seat and looked over at Quinlan.

Blink, she thought. *Blink, damn you.*

Quinlan stood up. He must have been expecting Smith to be recalled—Talon had not excused him and he was sitting in the back of the courtroom—but he obviously didn't expect the brevity and clarity of Smith's testimony.

"Cross-examination, Mr. Quinlan?" the judge asked.

"Um, uh," Quinlan stammered. "That is... Uh, no, Your Honor. No. No cross-examination. Thank you, Your Honor."

Quinlan sat down again. What else was he going to do? Cross was limited to responding to the questions asked on direct-examination. How could Quinlan respond to three questions without just reinforcing their answers?

"May the witness be excused now?" Judge Kalamaka asked.

"Yes, Your Honor," Talon answered first.

"No objection," Quinlan added without standing up.

Smith was finished, and so was Talon. "The defense rests, Your Honor," she said. "But we have a motion to renew. We would ask for a recess."

CHAPTER 38

Talon rushed over to Quinlan even as the jury was still filing out of the courtroom. Judge Kalamaka remained on the bench. After all, Talon had a motion to renew.

"Blink," Talon hissed at Quinlan. She had to stop herself from grabbing him by the lapels.

"What?" He looked thoroughly confused. Or maybe he was just still shell shocked from Smith's testimony.

"Blink," Talon repeated. "Concede. This trial is over. You heard Smith. You lost."

"I don't think I would say that exactly," Quinlan tried.

"*Your* cop just told *our* jury that *my* client told the truth," Talon boiled it down. "You cannot win."

"I can if they believe the other two officers," Quinlan argued.

Talon shook her head. "Really? That's where you're going to go with this? 'Ladies and gentlemen of the jury, please believe two of my cops, but not the third'? There is no way that is proof beyond a reasonable doubt."

"That's for the jury to decide," Quinlan insisted.

"We're going down that road?" Talon pressed. "Okay, well,

then guess what just became hugely relevant? Those personnel files I didn't get before. You're going to pit the word of one cop against another? Fine, let's see who the liars are? I think we both know the answer to that."

"You aren't necessarily going to get those personnel files," Quinlan responded, "just because the cops testified inconsistently."

"Small inconsistencies? I would agree," Talon said. " A huge 'everything they said was false' inconsistency? No, I'm getting those personnel files."

She turned and pointed at the judge's bench. The last juror was almost in the jury room. "Look at Kalamaka. He knows what I'm about to ask. And we both know he's going to grant it."

Quinlan pursed his mouth doubtfully.

"You and I both knew I wouldn't get them the first time I asked," Talon went on. "And we both know I'm going to get them now. Why the hell do you think I asked back then? Because I knew how this trial would go and I knew he wouldn't be able to say no twice, not after what just happened."

"You didn't know that was going to happen," Quinlan scoffed.

"I may not have known one hundred percent," Talon admitted, "but I planned for it. And now the only way those cops' personnel files don't see the light of day is if you dismiss."

"Dismiss?" Quinlan laughed. "Dismiss a charge of assault in the first degree against a police officer? How in the world do I explain that?"

Talon should have been able to give a speech about the higher ethics prosecutors are held to and should aspire to. How prosecutors represent all of the people, even the defendants. How prosecutors are supposed to, above all else, seek justice, not victory. And how sometimes justice requires dismissal. But that would never work with a prosecutor like Quinlan. She decided to get real.

"That's the beauty of it, Eric," Talon explained. "You're supposed to do the right thing. Seek justice and all that. But we both know you don't really do that. What you really do is protect cops. And the best way to protect those two cops is to keep me from seeing what's in their personnel files. Come on, Eric, you know me. You think that will be the end of it? You think I'll just read the files with a glass of Chablis and be satisfied with my little victory? No way. It's the first step in a journey of a thousand subpoenas. I'll get their files, then I'll get their supervisors' files. Shit, I'll probably get your personnel file before I'm done."

Quinlan's eyes widened a bit at that.

"Or," Talon suggested, "take the loss, blame Smith, make a speech about how prosecutors must stand on principle and justice and whatever bullshit you tell yourselves to fall asleep at night, and then dismiss. Tell the judge you concede that a jury can't find the charge beyond a reasonable doubt when one of your cops said it never happened, and dismiss the case."

Quinlan didn't respond. He was considering it.

"Then afterward, out of the courtroom, away from prying ears," Talon continued, "if those cops give you any shit, tell them you prevented their personnel files from going public. That will shut them up. You and I both know it will. You'll be a fucking hero."

The jurors were all safely away in the jury room and the bailiff closed the door behind them. It was time.

"I believe you said you had a motion to renew, Ms. Winter," Judge Kalamaka interrupted. "I believe I know what motion you were referring to and I am prepared to rule on it."

"Last chance, Eric," Talon whispered. "Lose the case, but win the war. Protect your cops. Be a hero."

Blink!

It was one thing to earn a win from a jury. It was another to get it from your opponent himself. To have the other side not only lose, but admit you had beaten them. To look you in the eye and blink. That was the ultimate win.

"Your Honor," Quinlan called out, "the State moves to dismiss the charges against the defendant."

And Talon had a passion for winning.

EPILOGUE

The celebration was had at *Delmonico's*, the strangely named Asian fusion restaurant on MLK Jr. Blvd., with the amazing food and, as it turned out, even better cocktails.

The celebration with Charlotte Draper, and even Jason Smerk. Not the celebration with Amelia Jenkins. That celebration had been in the courtroom, with hugs and tears and thank-yous. Celebrations with criminal defendants were intense, and they needed to stay separate. The intimacy of saving someone's life didn't translate well outside of the courtroom. Talon wasn't looking for new friends.

But she liked Charlotte Draper and she wanted to know the details behind the settlement Smerk had negotiated with Grainsley after Talon made him blink.

"The land has been put in trust," Draper explained, "to be transferred to the Tribe in twelve months, at which time, the Tribe will execute a leaseback to the yacht club for them to continue to operate and receive the revenue from their restaurant and hotel for the next ten years."

"So you get the land, they get the money, and Grainsley gets ten years to figure out what to do next," Talon summarized. "Win-

win-win."

"Yes, yes, yes," Draper agreed. "Thank you for forcing Grainsley to the table. I don't think we would have gotten to this result without you."

Talon raised an expectant eyebrow at Smerk.

He looked pained at the thought, but admitted it. "I suppose she's right. And I suppose you were too."

"It was a good result," Draper added. "A fair result."

"That's because," Curt spoke up from his seat next to Talon, "she has a passion for justice."

The celebration with Draper, Smerk, and Curt. He wanted to come along. She could hardly say no. He had helped with the case. He had found the restaurant. And there was that whole hooking up the night before trial thing. She had known that wasn't going to be able to be just a one-time thing. Not after their previous one-time thing.

Zack was one type of passion. Curt, apparently, was another.

"Oh, your drink is empty," Curt noticed, reaching out for Talon's glass. "I'll get you another one."

As he stood up, he leaned over to try to kiss Talon on the cheek, but she put a hand in his face and stopped the maneuver. "No."

Curt accepted the rebuke, grinned, and headed toward the bar.

"He's cute," Draper admired, watching after him. "How'd you two end up together?"

Talon sighed, but had to smile at herself. "I blinked."

END

THE TALON WINTER LEGAL THRILLERS

Winter's Law

Winter's Chance

Winter's Reason

Winter's Justice

Winter's Duty

Winter's Passion

THE DAVID BRUNELLE LEGAL THRILLERS

Presumption of Innocence

Tribal Court

By Reason of Insanity

A Prosecutor for the Defense

Substantial Risk

Corpus Delicti

Accomplice Liability

A Lack of Motive

Missing Witness

Diminished Capacity

Devil's Plea Bargain

Homicide in Berlin

Premeditated Intent

Alibi Defense

ALSO BY STEPHEN PENNER

Scottish Rite

Blood Rite

Last Rite

Mars Station Alpha

The Godling Club

ABOUT THE AUTHOR

Stephen Penner is an attorney, author, and artist from Seattle.

In addition to writing the *Talon Winter Legal Thrillers,* he is also the author of the *David Brunelle Legal Thriller Series,* starring Seattle homicide prosecutor David Brunelle; the *Maggie Devereaux Paranormal Mysteries,* recounting the exploits of an American graduate student in the magical Highlands of Scotland; and several stand-alone works.

For more information, please visit *www.stephenpenner.com.*

Made in the USA
Las Vegas, NV
21 August 2022